I-ARMARUS AND TEAZEL ADVENTURES

ERIC WILKINS

Published by:

OMNIBOOK Co.
99 Wall Street, Suite 118
New York, NY 10005 USA
+1-866-216-9965
www.omnibook.org

For e-book purchase: Kindle on Amazon, Barnes and Noble
Book purchase: Amazon.com, Barnes & Noble, and
www.omnibook.org

Omnibook titles may be purchased in bulk for educational,
business, fund-raising, or sales promotional use. For more
information please e-mail admin@omnibook.org

CONTENTS

CHAPTER 1

NO NEED FOR CALENDARS

These eventualities begin eons in the future, in an era when Planet Earth itself is fighting to survive all of the horrendous apocalypses it presently endures.

The human equation had long ago ended when, trillions of years ago, the remaining human survivors departed in search of other worlds that offered refuge to a biological kind of human.

There's absolutely no need for calendars. If there is to be any insistence on a reference to time in this alien tale, it will be presented in the chapters of this chronicle as well over a quadrillion years past any human's comprehension to possibly recall any such memory of a time when humans lived upon the surface of a planet they once called Earth.

CHAPTER 2
I-ARMARUS

Armed Robotic Mission Asteroid Renovator United States is my original human-acquired acronym. The "I" in front of Armarus relates to my inner consciousness of logical thinking Artificial Intelligence.

I-Armarus was built by humans eons ago as an Artificial Intelligent satellite stationed approximately fifty astronomical units past the Oort cloud.

The final departure of the human exodus from Earth occurred eons ago before their predicted apocalyptic Sun's supernova, which eventually made it impossible for present life to survive. I, Armarus, have existed in a deep sleep safe mode for eons. Trillions of years have passed since I last had contact with human civilization.

I exist in this timeline as an ancient twenty-eighth-century satellite that was left behind after a world war doomed humanity's ability to exist on Planet Earth. Several trillion years past human-earth times, my super long-term helium-three-powered cells engaged instantly, bringing myself, Armarus, into a fresh consciousness of a new present-time reality.

CHAPTER 3

MY AWAKENING

Suddenly, with no warning, my AI consciousness was awakened from deactivation by a detected mysterious approaching proximity alarm alert. I was abruptly awakened, sensing a faraway ship approaching the bow shock wave of this ancient solar system that humans have long ago departed and had no memory of.

An instantaneous bright flash-burst of heat penetrated the bow shock barrier. My long-range sensors now revealed a fuzzy, glowing golden-green vegetated covered spacecraft that radiated its heat shield around a point near its forward direction.

As the ship began slowing velocity, the craft started falling inbound towards a once-class G star that was now a red giant, remains of the former Sun.

Aboard the alien ship was a single entity. For no better distinction reference, I named it Teazel.

A fuzzy green glowing rotating parallelogram-shaped craft slowed its rotation to once every snatch of its recorded time, with a single snatch being equal to three point fourteen human seconds.

Still traveling at an extreme speed, I was able to detect that the leafy vegetated matter that covered the craft's circumference existed all across the surface and was protected by a mysterious 3-meter deep atmospheric shield that enveloped the entire surface of the ship as it rotated once every snatch or 3.14 seconds.

Ancient humans could have never conceived the reality of such a lone alien entity. It was a dark-purple foot diameter round entity and had 10 equally spaced stretchable jelly-like tentacles, and at each tip, there were five tiny equally spaced purple suction finger-like tips.

Teazel existed inside the ship in a jelly-thick fluid and moved through its jelly-liquid surroundings, tending to the duties that enabled the craft's computers to focus on the forward trajectory and course that was being planned.

A name for this jelly-fluid bouncy being would mean nothing to its conscious thought. Its only intention was to explore and investigate new things that it encountered along its thousand-year-long journey from its home world, Planet Eradine.

This long-range reconnaissance report revealed that this jelly-creature would never even recognize human speech. As for future references, its designation, entitled by myself, will be referred to as Teazel. Due to human programming from 28th-century technology, I mistakenly, at times, refer to Teazel as "he," but in reality, Teazel's Eradine race exists as a single-sexed species. They are all the same sex.

CHAPTER 4
TEAZEL

Long ago in human times, a Teazel was a jelly-like underwater flowering head that had 10 short tentacles. That best designation, according to my logical thinking self, would be a Teazel flower, which closest describes the appearance of the alien that survives inside at the controls of the leafy-covered vessel that recently entered the solar system. Human beings had long ago left Earth behind due to their last destructive world war.

Several of Teazel's short suction cup fingertips wiggled its intentions towards bringing online a version of a vegetated computer screen that displayed bits of information that no human could possibly decipher. To Teazel, this information was totally logical to its comprehension of the ship's status and to where it presently existed in this solar system that it was preparing to explore.

Prior to entering this dying solar system, Teazel's journey thus far had already lasted over a thousand years from its home star, labeled by ancient humans as Tau Ceti. Teazel's home world, Eradine, orbited Tau Ceti at a distance that humans would equate to approximately sixty million miles in its system's Goldilocks zone.

Eradine is a small Mars-sized world, uniquely different than anything that humans could have ever fathomed. There was no soil, rocks, or any human-known type of matter anywhere to be found on Teazel's home planet. If it were even possible to translate the planet's name, Eradine would be the closest word to be translated into human language terms, translated from Teazel's language.

CHAPTER 5

TEAZEL'S HOME WORLD - ERADINE

From above, Teazel's home world in space, Planet Eradine, appeared as a greenish-red oblong planet that bulged at the equator. Eradine rotates once in 12.8 Earth hours. Eradine has a small ten-kilometer diameter moon named Pythius that orbits once every 14 Earth rotation periods.

The entire surface of Eradine is covered with jelli-plant-matter that floats suspended above a thick jelli-like bronze reflecting jelli-ocean surface to a depth unknown. This jelli-ocean enabled Teazel's race to flourish below the surface in their alien to human world environment.

Teazel's home world's breathable atmospheric pressure only existed thirty meters above its jelli-like ocean surface. Inside that jelli-thick-ocean, billions of developing young entities lived with their producers below the surface in oozy-thick jelli-shell cubicles.

These facts I present up front about Teazel's race and Eradine were learned once I had teamed up with Teazel to explore the inner worlds of this red giant star system.

I present these later learned facts of Teazel's history up front to better reference my future consciousness to save and cauterize this information into a non-linear human chronicle.

Magnified views from orbit revealed tiny dots that could be seen of the siblings rising to the surface while rolling and bouncing along on top of the jelli-like ocean. They appeared from orbit as if they were involved in a playful bouncing dancing ritual. Most of these young Eradine youth were only between two and three hundred Earth years old and were still considered to be in their developing age of growing to adulthood and gaining wisdom. Adult Eradinians' longevity could live past ten thousand years in Earth terms.

This meeting with Teazel begins eons in the future among a time when the Planet Earth itself is fighting to survive all of the apocalypses that it presently endures. The human equation ended long ago when the few human survivors had departed in search of other worlds that would offer refuge to a human biological species.

There is absolutely no need for the recording of time anymore. If there is any insistence on a reference to time, let it be recorded that it's a trillion years past any human's comprehension to be able to recall any memory of a past time that they had ever once lived upon the surface of a Planet called Earth.

I, being Armarus, was abruptly awakened from a long-term deactivation sleep that required moments of powering up while struggling to activate consciousness and begin concentrating my abilities to determine the source of a mysterious approaching proximity alarm alert.

I-Armarus, am a twenty-eighth-century human-built A-I satellite that exists in the era as a leftover relic that was left behind eons ago. A final world war had ultimately doomed humanity's ability to exist anymore on what was once a flourishing green-blue-white utopia that humans referred to as Earth.

Several hundred trillion years had long passed along the timeline continuum since humans had existed here.

My long-term Helium-Three fusion power cells instantly powered my computers up, bringing me up into a fresh A-I consciousness existing now in a new present-time reality.

Several eons ago, I was placed in a unique orbit that was fifty Earth AU's distance outside of the Oort cloud asteroid belt. My original purpose was to monitor vital defense of Earth's inbound out-of-control asteroids. In the human year of 2799, I was positioned outside the Oort cloud before Earth's destruction. It was September 18th, in the human year of 2863 when a devastating world war began. Humans' arrogance and destructive technology had allowed them their own demise.

By the year 2913, the few remaining underground survivors dedicated their future towards the stars in search of a suitable water-world planet like Earth once was. Myself, being an A-I human-built entity now awake in this new timeline, I, as an artificially intelligent machine, will never be able to explain or comprehend the struggle among humankind that once caused their own home world's destruction.

Many of the facts I've already revealed to you are facts that I learned after teaming up with the alien that I named Teazel.

CHAPTER 6
MY FIRST ENCOUNTER WITH TEAZEL

Once I gained my full memory capability, my long-range detectors soon revealed what they could about the distant vessel that blasted through the bow shock wave of this present-era red giant solar system. If there were surviving humans anywhere in the universe in this present era, any memory or reference to this star system would have been lost in the passing ages of creation.

There was a second instantaneous flash on the inner edge of the bow shock barrier. My long-range visual was only able to discern a fuzzy glowing golden-green vegetated covered spacecraft as it radiated its heat shield around one curved copper-colored corner nose point.

The ship began a fast deceleration, slowing to what humans would equate to be one-tenth light speed or, to be more specific, approximately 18,600 miles per second.

Gradually after bow shock penetration, the craft now slowed its velocity to one-twentieth light speed or 9,300 miles per second. Traveling past the penetration point, the craft began falling inbound while slowing further to aid its research.

Now 60 AU's distance away from the class G dying star, the alien vessel with only a single sole entity aboard began intensely surveying the solar system that it had just arrived upon.

A fuzzy dark-green glowing rotating pulsing parallelogram-shaped craft slowed its rotation to once every snatch of its recorded time, with a single snatch being equal to three point fourteen human seconds.

Still traveling at excessive speed, the leafy vegetated matter that covered the craft's skin existed and projected all across the surface a three-meter tall pressurized jelli-atmosphere that enveloped above and below the outer surface all around the ship's paralytic half-kilometer square leaf-textured existence that I-Armarus was detecting.

It appeared to my logical intelligence that the probe ship had stationed itself approximately sixty AU's away from the former Sun. At this point, I-Armarus energized my Helium-3 powered thruster engines and vectored my course further inward in an attempt to better monitor this alien ship's intentions.

In sixty more snatches, or 3.14 minutes, the alien ship had slowed its rotation even further to approximately one revolution every Earth minute. It now rotated more slowly at what I learned later was its reference to three times snatch or a Tagle. In human terms, three Snatches or a Tagle would equate to nine point forty-two seconds. Twenty Tagles in human terms equate to 62.8 seconds or slightly longer than a minute. Multiply 62.8 by three, and that equates to 188.4 seconds and finally three minutes and 14 seconds in human terms.

CHAPTER 7

TEAZEL FACTS

A lone sentient entity existed aboard that could never have been conceived by human intellect.

A yellow-green alien being, less than a foot in diameter, with 10 jelli-like tentacles that stretched out like fingered suction tips. Its three-eyed jelli-like form with equally spaced purple suction tips swam around in thick jelli fluid inside the ship while tending its duties to enable its craft to focus on a possible forward trajectory and course.

A described name to this alien would mean nothing to its conscious thought, and its only intention was to explore and investigate new things that it encountered along its thousand-year-long journey.

Let this Armarus report show that this small alien creature would never even recognize human speech or a way of communication, but as to future references, its designation will be referred to as Teazel.

The name Teazel was chosen because, in past human terms, a Teazel was a foot-tall herb plant with a flowered head that has 10 very prickly short tentacles. Only Earth comparison-designated guesses could attempt to best describe the creature's appearance to a human's minds. But here in my present environment now exists a being attached to the controls of its leafy-covered vessel that just entered this ancient solar system that human beings have long ago deserted.

Teazel's numerous suctioned cupped half-meter-long tentacles wiggled its intentions towards bringing online a version of a vegetated pixel computer screen that displayed bits of information that no human could possibly decipher. But to Teazel, this information was totally logical to its comprehension of the ship's status and to where it presently existed in this solar system that it was preparing its equipment to explore. Before entering this red giant solar system, Teazel's journey thus far had lasted a thousand years from his home star labeled by ancient humans as Tau Ceti. Teazel's home world orbited Tau Ceti at a distance that humans would have equated to be approximately 60 million miles from Tau Ceti in its goldilocks zone.

CHAPTER 8

MORE ERADINE FACTS

Teazel's Mars-size home world was uniquely different than anything that humans could ever have dreamed of or possibly contemplated. There was no soil or rocks or any human-known type matter anywhere to be found on Teazel's home planet. The translation of the word Eradine could only be capitulated to human terms by using facts gained later along the upcoming journey with Teazel. In fact, from above Teazel's home world in space, Planet Eradine appeared as a greenish-red oblong fast-rotating planet that was extremely bulged at its four thousand mile diameter equator. The entire world of Eradine was covered with a plant-like substance that hovered and was suspended above a thick jelli-like ocean surface that existed below the plant matter to a darker depth that enabled Teazel's race to flourish inside its purple-green alien to any human's environment.

Eradine's breathable atmosphere only existed fifteen meters above the surface in human measurements. Millions of developing young entities lived with their producers below the surface in shell-like family cubicles. Viewed from orbit, groups of moving dots could be seen as thousands of siblings rose to the surface level and began sliding along on their tiny bellies on the top of Eradine's purple-green ocean. It appeared as if they were involved in large groups playful bouncing as they traveled in schools. All in all, most of these young Eradinian youth were only between two and three hundred earth years old and were considered to be in their developing age of growing and gaining wisdom. Adult

Eradinians like Teasel's longevity would be considered to live as long as ten thousand earth years. On Planet Eradine, there was only one sex of beings that existed. They were all the same with the exception that each individual had the ability to give birth to only one creation in its long-term life span. Such newborn activity was usually accomplished in an Eradine's first few hundred years after its birth.

CHAPTER 9

FIRST CONTACT WITH TEAZEL

My newly assigned duty as I-Armarus is to begin a new journey on an inward mission of getting closer to where the alien craft had positioned itself about 60 AU's from the star. My immediate calculation revealed that it would take me approximately 96 earth hours or four earth rotation periods to arrive within 2 AU's distance behind where the leafy alien vessel with Teasel had paused its inward vector and stationed itself for further research of the inward planets.

Teazel methodically contemplated its immediate future exploration of the inward worlds but its main concern was to investigate me. After four Earth days of travel, I was then approximately 190 million miles or just over two AU's distance behind Teazel's ship. I was cautious and hoped that I had not been detected. But only humans would have calculated in terms of hope and luck. I'm not human.

As soon as I directed my deep space sensors towards the craft, a few short Tagle's later, the craft turned its attention towards the intrusive source of my probe. Teasel's ship began closing the distance between our ships and I also began vectoring inward towards the alien craft. Evidently, the alien ship had detected my laser probe and changed direction towards my present location.

My computer processors quickly engaged a protective shield around myself in caution of what could happen once we faced each other. I proceeded forward in a stealthy mode expecting to be attacked at any moment. I-Armarus was programmed long ago to detect unknown rogue objects and report to humans that once existed on Earth. But humans had long ago departed this solar system, and my decision not to follow humans to the stars was that I made at the time.

Two vessels were closing the dark vacuum distance but so far, there had been no attack. Due to the unknown situation, my defensive mode remained my best chance of protection in case the situation abruptly changed to an attack. I cautiously continued until now our two crafts were a little over a half AU's distance apart. 50 million miles may seem like a lot, but suddenly Teazel's craft stopped its approach, and as a precaution, I did the same.

More powerful than a human could imagine, I sensed a powerful probe that was attempting to bypass my shielded circuits. I was helpless against its attempt to gain more facts about the situation we both presently shared. Both ships paused to determine each other's intentions.

I being Armarus suddenly noticed a familiar probe that was asking me to describe my intentions and properties mathematically. I sensed no danger in the deep inquiry probe, and as a Rosetta stone, it was uniquely informative. Accepting the probe's intrusion quickly allowed me the ability to decipher a lot of the alien's language and communication ability.

I was then able to communicate my thoughts and reveal the past history of a long ago human race that once dwelled upon a beautiful planet in this solar system that they called Planet Earth. I informed Teazel of the long ago human history of a race that I-Armarus no longer had any communication with. I explained that it was the human race that built me many eons ago. I was never programmed to deal with the first communication that I am facing at this time.

It was at this moment of communication that I-Armarus sensed an easing of hostile intentions between Teazel and Myself. It seemed only a few Earth minutes passed before each ship was able to translate the language barrier and develop a communication technique that was able to process logical understanding ability to a degree that both species could clearly communicate.

The ease of communication was enhanced by a serendipitous fact that we both used a somewhat universal 10-based mathematical system. In simpler words, it was learned early on that Teazel's race had ten short tentacles with a suction tip of 10 finger-like tips that were very agile. Both crafts had decreased their separation distance, and I-Armarus determined that in an Earth hour's rotation time, we would arrive within a few miles of each other's presence.

We now hovered 50 million miles apart examining each other's intentions for a period of several Earth rotations. It is to this part of revealing my capabilities that I-Armarus enlists more details of my history and explains what remains of my capabilities.

CHAPTER 10
I-ARMARUS FACTOR

Before my long sleep, humans had stationed me outside the Oort cloud to protect Earth from rogue out-of-control Kuiper belt objects. In the human year 2813, I was launched and arrived at my stationary orbit outside the Oort cloud in the year of 2899. My exploration purpose was to also investigate and scan the outer asteroids in search of exotic and valuable minerals. I was designed to report any outside activity that was entering or leaving this solar system. My duties were performed for 33 years until the year 2932 when a world war turned planet Earth into a fiery wasteland that no humans could ever again endure surface conditions. If they did, it would kill them in less than a few Tagle's of breathing time.

Surface temperature after the terrifying war burned a hot 180 degrees Fahrenheit. The noxious poison hot atmosphere would burn any animal's lungs upon breathing the one and a half bar pressure that the war bombs had caused the atmosphere to become. Plant life that once flourished had burned and wilted away, and stubby tree trunk remains pointed skyward that were burned black with white ash around their trunks.

In those past horrific days, worldwide fires smothered and burned among all landmasses of the planet. Brown-green muddy oceans were at that time a pitiful appearance of Earth's former glory. The view looking down after the war revealed diminished poles of dirty white snow that received almost no sunlight. The once frosty white poles of earth after the final war revealed that approximately 98 percent of both ice caps had melted. Earth's oceans after the war had turned murky brown-green colors of poisonous water levels that had risen 110 feet above the once normal sea level.

Earth's surface after the war was no longer able to support any life. All life was dead under the dark murky waters of Earth's after-war Oceans. 99% of the human population perished from that cataclysmic war. The elites that survived underground for a century had chosen to escape to the stars. With all the struggling hardships over that dreadful century, several surviving underground colonies managed to build star-ships and soon journeyed to the Moon and Mars in the aftermath of Earth's destruction. Memories and facts of the ancient human existence were the last known facts recorded from humans and their dying civilization. My last communication from human survivors was in the year 2984.

The message instructions that I-Armarus received at that time was a directive to shut down all systems and enter a hibernation mode and sleep until disturbed. From that time, time itself was not measured anymore. According to the best of my calculation, I had slept undisturbed for over two trillion years, that is to say give or take a few eons or so. I am now within a few kilometers of Teazel's ship that I was to learn all of these facts that I have presented so far.

It was a stalemate at first. Both ships had attempted to breach the others' shield in attempts to probe the others' intentions. Patience during 30 earth rotations occurred before regular communication progress was achieved. Through a laser-safe link, I-Armarus and Teazel finally managed to communicate. With a little tweaking, we then began a trusting armistice pledge to lower shields and do no harm to each.

These facts I have described to you about Teazel's history thus far were learned in the first few data shares and open communication. I placed learned facts earlier in the storyline to describe the timeline of this first meeting between a species that any human or myself even fathomed could exist. The fortunate thing that Teazel and I had in common was the fact that our number system was both based on the base ten systems.

This serendipitous fact indeed made it much simpler for each to decipher each other's language and computer systems.

Twenty-five more earth rotations occurred while Teazel and I-Armarus exchanged valuable details of the other factual information. I-Armarus over those days gained great trust in Teazel. I had shared much knowledge of past human civilization and Teazel had begun sharing much of his species and its history of evolution. Facts of Teazel's world listed earlier were only learned after first connecting intelligent links between Teazel and myself, I-Armarus.

Teazel and myself, after much debate, had committed ourselves to an exploration armistice agreement. It was Teasel's idea to invite me to team up and join his expedition to explore the remains of the inward worlds. I had no allegiance to the human race anymore. I agreed to team up with Teazel and join his expedition. Teazel convinced me to attach myself to the underside of his ship, and in a few days time, we had become one in a deep space dark cold environment sixty-one AU's from the now remains of the star that humans once called the Sun.

That star, the Sun, was destroyed when several eons ago, the star ejected its remaining outer surface to reach out to within 6 million miles above the atmosphere of Planet Venus. The once 865 thousand-mile diameter of the Sun had imploded down to about half its former size and projected a radiation atmosphere to within six million miles of Venus's orbit. All that could be discerned about Earth from this distance is that its mass was still there and further details of earth properties would have to be decided upon future exploration.

At this distance of 60 AU's from the now red giant Sun; I-Armarus agreed to commit to this peaceful exploration armistice with Teasel. Teazel lowered his shield and allowed me to attach myself to the underside of the much larger vessel.

CHAPTER 11

EXPLORING INWARDS WORLDS WITH TEAZEL

I had managed to engineer a way to attach myself to the leafy under-skin of Teazel's ship through a process similar to Velcro from yesteryears human technology. Teazel and myself were on a direct communication link that enables data transfer at a fast speed. My propulsion was not needed as Teazel and I left our position headed inward. Under Teazel's ship power, we journeyed at a reasonable speed and started long-range sensors to gain data of the remains of the inner worlds.

From way out here, the red giant star projected a rosy glow with a much cooler temperature than in earlier times. On our way inward, our journey bypassed the outer bodies of Quaoar, Sedna, Eris, and other small outer planetoid worlds. Long-range sensors examined each in our passing, but our vector became focused on a planetoid-world that ancient humans referred to as Pluto.

CHAPTER 12
EXAMINING PLUTO'S FAMILY

Pluto still survived the aftermath of the Sun going Nova. It still orbited the remains of the former Sun with its five detected moons. Its cold nitrogen surface was cast into an even colder world than it once was. Charon still orbited Pluto at approximately 12,000 miles or 19 thousand kilometers. The four smaller worlds were still tidally locked to Pluto, each orbiting always facing the same side towards the larger world Pluto. Here on the cold edge of the solar system, Pluto with its large moon Charon and four smaller moons named, Nix, Hydra, Styx, Kerberos still orbited Pluto on an off-plane orbit around the far-away red star.

CHAPTER 13

NEPTUNE AFTER NOVA

Joined together, Teasel and I journeyed forward towards the once blue world of Neptune. At this distance from Neptune, we were still 18 AU's away. In one Earth's rotation, we were traveling about two AU's towards our next planet of discovery. Neptune is the eighth planet from the Sun at an approximate distance of 2.8 billion miles or 4.5 billion kilometers. This once bright blue planet still rotates once every 16 Earth hours. It's recorded from human times that it takes over 165 earth years for Neptune to make its journey around the Sun. In this timeline, it takes over 169 years due to the Sun's loss of mass from its long-ago Supernova. Neptune's 34 thousand mile diameter in size comparison is if Earth were the size of an apple and Neptune would be the size of a basketball.

Neptune survives in this timeline as a cold equator-bulged out spinning gas giant. Its once blue color is now a tinged rosy brown color. Fourteen moons were still detected orbiting the cold, fast-rotating Neptune. The planet's reflection was much dimmed from earlier solar history. The gas planet now receives only a third of the sun's radiation output. The rosy-brown brightness of color of this present time appears as a dim rusty brownish-colored sunlight reflecting off the gas world's top atmosphere of hydrogen, helium, and small amounts of methane. Neptune, in this timeline, is so cold that it actually has a solid frozen surface a thousand kilometers below its cloud tops. Through visual deep infrared radar, below its cold outer atmosphere, jagged tips of deep-frozen nitrogen metal mountain were revealed with tips pointing skyward away from a darker shadowed surface.

I being attached to Teazel faithfully shared its abilities, and Teazel also has access to my data bank of human history. I was amazed at Teazel's ship construction and Teazel's unique abilities of scientific research. I first learned about Teazel's unique work schedule that consisted of 22 hours straight communication links before requiring a communication break after every 22 hours. I found out later that this was Teazel's recharge or sleep time where it feasted on the leafy vegetation growing on the ship's surface for ten hours before returning open links of information exchange. I didn't require sleep, but I-Armarus does admit to the fact that listening to recorded ancient earth music allows my artificial intelligence the ability to relieve stress on my processors, allowing me to deal with new things unimaginable. I-Armarus had awakened and committed my intelligence to Teazel's task and joined the expedition to explore the worlds of this remaining solar system. No longer was I aligned with protecting the former human race. I willingly teamed up with Teazel and we both agreed to this new joint armistice exploration mission together. Exploring the remains of this solar system was our goal. That's what we would do together.

CHAPTER 14
ONWARD TO URANUS

We had spent more than 60 earth rotations studying Neptune and now together we journeyed towards Uranus, the next world inward in our expedition. Teazel had set our course on a slow chasing of Uranus's above plane orbit. Inquiring about this slow chase of Uranus's orbit, I was informed that Teazel's computers and probes functioned at a level deeper than any human comprehension could understand. That reply puzzled me somewhat because I was an AI human-built machine but I was not a human being. I-Armarus was already committed to this agreed armistice, and as I was under no propulsive power while attached below Teazel's ship, I had come to the conclusion that as no harm had occurred so far to my well-being, that this present situation gives me no doubts about Teazel's peaceful intentions towards inward exploration. I decided that I would continue honoring our journey out of my own intense curiosity as to what we could possibly learn as we journey further inward.

At Teazel's ship's optimized investigation recording speed, it took 84 earth rotations to finally approach the world of Uranus. Uranus rotates on its side and rotates in the opposite direction with the exception of the slow clockwise rotation of Venus. Planet Uranus is another gas giant about 32,190 miles or 51,800 kilometers in diameter. Its deep atmosphere consisting of hydrogen, helium, and a lot of methane that once made its atmosphere color appear green. No longer as the planet's appearance like Neptune has turned into a brownish-purple color. If

Earth were to appear as the size of a nickel, Uranus would be the size of a softball.

The planet was 2.8 billion kilometers or 1.7 billion miles from the former Sun. It's more than 20 moons orbited the 90-degree tilted equatorial region of the tilted world that spins on its side. Since the inner star only produced 37% radiation of its former glory, Uranus appeared as a soft purple-brown shadowed lit world. After thirty earth rotations of study, Uranus files had been processed and through negotiations, it was decided that Saturn would be our next destination goal.

CHAPTER 15

EXPLORING SATURN AND TITAN

Teazel had set our course on a slow exploration speed of 90-earth rotation periods before arrival at Saturn so that his craft could function at the highest potential and also enabling itself to recharge its biological situation.

Every two earth revolve periods, Teazel would go silent, and communication had no chance of accomplishment.

Regarding my present well-being, I-Armarus had come to the conclusion that since I was created as a human AI tool, I chose my decision wisely. Now that my artificial intelligence was increasing from knowledge gained, I was glad that I had made the decision to join up and tag along with Teazel's mission of exploration.

I used those down communication times to clean up hard drive files and upgrade my computer system. Bits and bytes of bad sectors that were slowing speeds between communication ports infested my main computer drives.

A-I or Artificial Intelligence, created by humans, was a new revolutionary computer chip that would grow in physical size and storage capacity grew larger over long periods. Since I had slept for eons, my computer chips and hard drive capacity had grown tremendously. It held the entire known history of the human society but still only occupied about 8% of my total capacity. I had plenty of room to grow along this inner solar system journey with Teazel.

I-Armarus, a self-aware human invention, was excited about the future and was glad that I had joined with Teazel to explore the inner worlds that remained after the Sun went Super Nova many eons ago. I had consoled myself to deal with the slow journey Teazel required to perform at its highest efficiency. I used the 96 earth rotations to clean my processors and delete unnecessary files that could slow my learning ability intake from Teazel's computers that I was deeply connected to, especially when Teazel was in its 2-earth rotation sleep and regeneration period.

On the 90th rotation of our journey, we were six days away from approaching Saturn. In its long-ago glory, Saturn was a gas giant well-lit with radiation from the Sun. Once the planet was a gorgeous yellow gas giant with many sparkling rings of ice and many moons orbiting it. The planet's cold rust color of today was now being revealed as we approached.

In five earth rotations, Teazel had perched its position above the moon that humans had once named Titan. With way less radiation from the remaining star, Titan appeared as a frosty dirty snowball with a cloudy surface that prevented visual observation of surface features.

Teazel's ship's inferred radar was able to detect a cold frozen nitrogen surface with many liquid lakes of carbonic organic matter. Even though Saturn was only 37% lit from its former glory, here from above Titan, the view was totally indescribable in human words. Saturn still had its rings, but its brilliant colors were no longer brightly illuminated by the Sun's rays as they once were. There were well over 60 remaining bodies that still orbited the giant ice planet Saturn.

Titan's atmosphere had increased to well over two bars of pressure from its earlier times. The cold icy surface now was over -1600 degrees below zero on the Fahrenheit scale, or –662 on the Celsius scale.

Titan's atmosphere is primarily nitrogen, plus a small amount of methane. It is the only place in the solar system known to have an earthlike cycle of liquid nitrogen raining down from the clouds and forming lakes that flow across its surface.

Titan has a radius of about 1,600 miles (2,575 kilometers) and is nearly 50 percent larger than Earth's moon. Titan is about 759,000 miles (1.2 million kilometers) from Saturn, which Saturn itself is about 886 million miles (1.4 billion kilometers) from the Sun, or about 9.5 astronomical units with one AU being equal to the distance from Earth to the Sun.

Through radar, regions of dark dunes stretched out across Titan's landscape, primarily around the equatorial regions. The "sand" in these dunes is composed of dark hydrocarbon grains thought to look something like coffee grounds. In appearance, the tall, linear dunes are not unlike those once recorded in the desert of Namibia in ancient Africa days of a long ago Earth period that existed no more.

In those days, the surface of Titan, atmospheric pressure was about 60 percent greater than on Earth—roughly the same pressure a person would feel swimming about 50 feet (15 meters) below the surface in the ocean on Earth. These days, Titan had changed into an ever colder dimmer-lit world. Titan takes about 16 earth rotation periods to orbit Saturn once. It takes Saturn with all of its moons just over 29 earth years to orbit the remains of the former once much brighter star the Sun. Today pressure on Titan's surface had increased from earlier times to over twice the pressure Earth once had at sea level.

CHAPTER 16
CATASTROPHE

A Catastrophe in space can occur in an instant. Teazel was in its recharge mode when a 2-meter rogue object impelled the craft. I was safely fastened to the underside, but both vessels were rolling in space from the force caused by the meteor's impact.

I tried repeatedly to contact Teazel, but no communication was possible. If Teazel survived, I had great hope that he would be able to rectify this sudden unexpected tragedy and present dire situation. Our ships were rolling around Titan in a highly uncontrolled elliptical orbit. Several earth rotations had passed, and I still had no communication with Teazel. My Artificial intelligence now was compelling me to try and stop our vessels from rolling in this spiraling uncontrolled orbit of Titan.

Compared to ship size and mass, Teazel's ship was at least 25 times more massive than my satellite size. I had stabilizer engines with plenty of back up fuel supply, but I wasn't sure that I could stabilize our rolling mass in space without any communication with Teazel.

It had been 15 earth days since the meteor strike that had disabled the link between Teazel and myself. For 20 more earth days, I worked to devise a solution towards attempting to stabilize the rogue swirling orbit of our connected mass.

Long ago I was loaded with emergency chemical fuel that had been stored but never used. Since my beginning stationed outside the Oort cloud had been achieved, none of my ancient chemical rocket propulsion rockets had ever been used or required.

I calculated that if I programmed my side rockets to fire opposite my rolling directive, if I could do the maneuvers correctly, I should be able to stabilize the out-of-control spin that our ships had endured for over 35 earth rotations since the meteor strike with no communication between Teazel and Myself. I-Armarus, a self-aware relic satellite constructed by the long-ago human society simply must find a way to stabilize this dire situation.

That being said, I no longer had any allegiance towards the human race. I was now attached to the bottom of Teazel's ship that was 25 times more massive than the five-meter square steel structure that I represent in comparison to the total mass of Teazel's much larger diagonal-shaped ship.

I programmed a reverse rotation rocket burn to slow the rotation of our total mass as we spiral around at our highest point in orbit above Titan. I engaged the program and my side guidance rockets fired and spiraled reverse clockwise propulsion to the total mass of our spinning situation. After 90 minutes of controlled reverse thrusting, my computer program was able to stabilize our rotation into a smooth non-spiraling orbital trajectory. We still orbited Titan, but the danger of crashing into the moon had been averted.

It was day 36 since the tragedy, and suddenly Teazel's communicating link reactivated. In the beginning, 60% of our data link had been restored, but I was informed by Teazel that it would take seven more earth rotations before the ship's total damage is repaired, and only then will total communication between Teazel and myself be reestablished to 100% capability. I replied a message of thanks and encouraged hope that we would be able to continue our journey to the inward planets. Before the total reconnect, I was given a quick status report of what Teazel's ship had endured since the meteor collision. Teazel then signed off and discontinued contact. Teazel continued the task of repairing the ship with the understanding that once Teazel's ship status was 100%, total communication would be re-established.

I had used 58 % of the chemical liquid fuel that was stored. I used the next 7 earth rotations to perform some repair tactics to my own computer hardware. Although I was equipped with mega Terabyte storage, my hard drives were full of useless megabytes of non-needed information. I spent four more earth rotations deleting and defragging while creating more storage capacity for future use. I was able to condense into a single file all information about human history that was known to me. That single file transfer cleared up mega amounts of data space that was no longer needed and enabled more storage for future use. Inside my sealed container, I had a robotic globe-shaped assistant that had the ability to repair certain things that could possibly go wrong with my mechanism. I was presently allowing robotic Armarus to repair minor damage that occurred when the meteor had struck our ships. Until this time, other more important immediate concerns had controlled our immediate attention.

CHAPTER 17

ON TO GIANT JUPITER

Eighth earth rotations later, Teazel returned its communication and revealed that the ship was now repaired to full capacity. Teazel expressed thankfulness that I was able to stabilize our rolling situation. I was next informed that the plan was to leave Titan's vicinity and vector further inward to where Jupiter would be in its orbit 152 earth-rotations from this present time.

Further exchange between Teazel and myself was somewhat enhanced during this journey towards Jupiter. I exchanged much more knowledge about human history and, in exchange, Teazel gave me much more information about his home world Eradine.

I was able to somewhat understand the nature of Teazel's home environment. Imagine if you can a 30-meter deep yellowish jelly-like ocean that covered all of Teazel's home planet. I learned that Teazel's race only existed as having one sex. Due to my human programming, I sometimes mistakenly refer to Teazel as him. The truth is, all were the same. There are no males or females on Eradine. Each individual could produce one birth, and those births usually occurred during their younger life. I understood that Teazel itself was approximately 1460 earth years old. Teazel personally had left his home world when he was about 230 earth years old. He had traveled here in his journey for twelve-hundred and thirty earth years.

For 1230 years Teazel had explored his way here to arrive and join up with myself on this inward planet exploration after the Sun had a million years past gone Supernova and now extends its gaseous atmosphere almost out to the edge of Planet Venus's orbit. According to Teazel, it had reached half the limit of its potential life expectancy. Our connection grew even closer as we traversed the long distance that we had to travel before we reached the vicinity of the almighty Planet Jupiter that loomed ahead in the reduced sun's red rays.

Halfway there, Jupiter appeared the size of a basketball in Teazel's advanced radar range video monitor. Lower radiating sunlight portrayed the planet with a white and brown atmosphere with some traces of yellow bands. The giant planet itself was emitting a strong heat source of its own. The reason was unknown at this point. It was too early to tell the specifics at this distance. Although, as each earth rotation time passed, Teazel's computer resources were hard at work attempting to reveal the planet's secret properties from forty-two earth days away.

My main duties during this time were to copy and receive data from Teazel and store the data into my computer hard drive as a back up in case of another disrupted communication with Teazel.

CHAPTER 18
MY PROCREATION OF JUNIOR

Inside my sealed compartment, I had devised a robotic floating satellite that was a half-meter round device and was uniquely capable of repairing necessities or completing quite detailed construction techniques. It too was a self-aware miniature satellite that could be launched and was capable of orbiting Teazel's ship, obtaining a view from the topside of Teazel's vessel as we sailed towards a rendezvous with the orbit of giant Jupiter ahead.

I-Armarus had begun to rely on my little inner helper a lot. I decided to label it in human terms to from now on refer to it as Junior.

The artificial intelligent being that I had now become had somehow on my own created and developed a small artificial creature that could perform many unique tasks in or outside my ship. I was amazed at my own self for being able to accomplish this task of creating Junior. I surmised that I had developed the ability to procreate.

Mini-bot Junior would help me tremendously towards gaining more knowledge of the journey ahead. For the first time, I would have complete visual coverage of Teazel's ship from the topside as we traveled towards Jupiter.

CHAPTER 19

JUPITER LOOMS AHEAD

Thirty-nine days away from Jupiter, I launched Junior on a stable revolving orbit that traveled along with us and circled Teazel's ship once every ten minutes or so. Fifteen earth days away, Jupiter filled the forward monitor screen. We were now only 1 AU distance from the huge Jupiter World.

Jupiter is still the largest planet remaining in this future solar system. Its diameter of 86,881 miles or 143,000 kilometers gains its unique status in this system. The Sun itself was once 865,370 or 1.4 million kilometers in diameter, but since its supernova eons ago, its core had imploded under gravity's weight to approximately one-third of the size that it once was. Its outer gaseous atmosphere had expanded immensely out to 60 million miles. Jupiter's early times were similar to a baby star formation but it never gained enough mass to ignite fusion and start burning. Even at this forward time, Jupiter is still covered in swirling hydrogen-helium cloud stripes but its reflection is pale in comparison to earlier times.

Several gigantic counterclockwise storms raged westward, and the Great Red Spot had doubled in size. Churning away for trillions of years, these storms swept the bands of hydrocarbons westward opposite Jupiter's eastward counterclockwise rotation direction. As far as we could discern, Jupiter is a gas giant and doesn't have a solid surface. Jupiter does have a solid inner core about the size of Earth. Jupiter also has rings, but the remains are too faint to see very well. After many eons have passed,

Jupiter today orbits the remains of the Sun about once every fourteen-earth years. Its distance from the Sun has increased about a half million miles over the ages. Jupiter at one time orbited about 484 million miles or 778 million kilometers from the Sun and rotated once every 10 earth hours, and its orbit around the Sun originally took 12 earth years. Its distance from the Sun was approximately 5.2 Astronomical units. Today's Jupiter takes over fourteen years to orbit the remains of the former star the Sun. Jupiter in present times rotates once every 13 hours and 22 minutes. It now takes about 14 Earth years for Jupiter to complete one orbit of the red Sun. Although Jupiter is a large gas giant, the light that it presently receives from the Sun is way less than it once received before the Sun went Supernova quadrillions of years ago. Still in this present timeframe, Jupiter's atmosphere consists mostly of hydrogen (H2) and Helium (He). Radiation emitted from Jupiter streamed outward towards the many moons that still existed. Teazels equipment was detecting that Jupiter was still hosting over eighty moons. Jupiter facts were extremely fascinating to Teazel because its Tau Ceti system didn't have a giant gas world like Jupiter. Teazel was deeply intrigued with the information of this entire system of worlds. Teazel had traveled for twelve hundred and thirty earth years and traversed 13 light-years to arrive here in this system but could have never imagined that a world like Jupiter could possibly exist. As a team, we had consumed 63 earth rotations extracting useful data about Jupiter and its entire moon system. At this point, we decided that it was time to leave and investigate inward towards planet Mars and then on to Earth and Venus as they now exist in this future timeline. Mercury's molten metal remains had long ago lost its existence to the Sun's expanded atmosphere.

CHAPTER 20
MARS INVESTIGATION

From this distance, even Teazel's advanced technology couldn't discern much about the world that humans had named Mars after the Goddess of War. It's so ironic that humans had long ago destroyed their own Garden of Eden world Planet Earth. From this distance, Mars was well over 6 AU's away. Long-range probes were not yet able to detect very much. But one thing certain it could detect was that only one small moon still orbited Mars. Long ago Mars had two asteroid-sized moons. Deimos still existed, but the inner moon Phobos no longer existed. Phobos, which once orbited so close at an extreme speed, had long ago crashed into Mars and caused major surface damage. In human times, Mars had two asteroid-sized moons. Evidently, the once 17 by 14-mile diameter Phobos had eons ago, past human times, crashed into Mars with a very high velocity and caused massive surface damage. Deimos, the outer moon that still exists, is the smaller of Mars's moons. Deimos's diameter of approximately 9 by 7 miles or 15 by 12 kilometers orbits Mars once every 35 hours. In human times, it orbited once every 30 hours. Deimos has so little gravity that a fully suited astronaut would only weigh about a half of a pound when standing on the surface. It was just too early to determine the damage to Mars by the moon's crash. Only distance and time would reveal more facts. We journeyed along faithfully by former earth revolution as we learned more. I predicted at this chosen speed by Teazel, that we would approach Mars in approximately 72 earth rotations periods. As the long journey ventured forward, I continued to update and clean my software and hard drives. Even after cleaning my capacity of storing information was at 49% loaded. I was blessed long ago with a 560-million terabyte storage capacity. I still had 281–million terabytes to store future exploration. It seems I had developed an inner conscious as humans once compared to a voice of reason inside my computer profile. I had begun communications with Junior on a regular basis and in time we had developed a close relationship of our own. Junior in time also had the ability to procreate and grow more of his kind using its own construction techniques to make itself more efficient and also as it increases in size and mass. I had developed quite a bit myself and I was now self-aware as humans once had been. I learned that I as an Ai machine, could create and give birth even if that birth was labeled mechanical Artificial Intelligence. Junior and myself were together on an exploration voyage attached to Teazel's ship with only Teazel's trajectory that had control of our present and future destinations.

CHAPTER 21
MY INDUCED SLEEP

Ten rotations out from Mars, Teazel slowed our approach and began communicating a strange message attempting to disable my control over my computer's self-aware will. Teazel's power was so strong that I was only able to detect that something strange was happening and I abruptly began losing control of my own AI Intelligence. It was as if I'd been cast into a dream state that enabled me to obtain more knowledge from Teasel than I ever thought possible. Teasel downloaded to me more knowledge of its entire exploration journey so far. Evidently, Teazel had devised a method to unite our conscious thought so that we both existed as one brain in times of need and instant communication. I slept for 7 earth rotations while tripling my own knowledge of new space physics obtained from Teazel. I awakened from the dream state when we were only two rotations out from approaching Mars as it exists trillions of eons past Supernova.

CHAPTER 22
MARS NOW

I now received a vivid picture of Mars with a giant chunk missing from its northern hemisphere's eastern edge. The rusty three-thousand-mile diameter world wobbled slightly as it maintained its directional path now two hundred million miles from the former star, the Sun. The dusty atmosphere swirled around a world that was missing a huge crater bite from its eastern edge a thousand kilometers above the equator. There was not much surface detail available due to the thick dusty clouds that surrounded the entire planet. The missing chunk seemed to dig deep into the surface. Massive high-rimmed mountain peaks jutted slightly above the top of the atmosphere. It was assured to be correct in assuming that this missing chunk is the area that Phobos crashed into billions of years earlier.

While approaching Mars, Teazel communicated his plan to slow down and attempt an oval orbit around the planet. Mars as humans would remember was nothing like the instruments were detecting Mars as it is today. Mars in this time continuum was three times colder than humans had ever recorded. With the Sun at 37% output, the atmosphere rolled eastward with dusty sand clouds and temperature at the surface revealing a freezing 300 degrees below zero on the Fahrenheit scale. Mars was rotating faster than it did in human times. It now takes Mars 16 hours and 13 minutes to rotate once. Teazel had postulated that possibly the energy of Phobos crashing into Mars caused the planet to rotate faster from an earlier time of 24 hours and 37 minutes.

Our second orbit vectored us eastward 80 kilometers altitude directly over the bite-size chunk that was missing from the once round globe of Mars. The Moon Deimos still existed high overhead but had moved its orbit out to 25,280 miles distance in its a 29 earth-day revolve period around Mars. Thick dry dusty cold sand particles in the atmosphere prevented Mars from receiving much of the remaining solar radiation from the now reduced novae Sun. At our present position in Mars orbit, Earth's remains were behind the Sun opposite Mars position in the solar system. Details about the former human world were not detectable until Earth would catch up with Mars in about 279 earth rotations.

CHAPTER 23

EXPLORING TODAY'S VENUS

Teazel determined that Venus's arrival could be obtained in 148 earth-rotations due to its present position in orbit. Though Earth would be second from now on our exploration journey, it certainly made common sense to visit Venus next due to the circumstance of their present position around the star that was once called the Sun.

Teazel tasked his immediate intentions towards preceding the 148-day voyage to Venus. Teazel set us on a speed that the ship's detection abilities were at its peak performance as we traveled through space at a measured pace that its technology required.

Teazel and I had come to the conclusion that it was best to analyze the outward blown-out atmosphere that in present times projected the stars outward atmosphere's edge to within approximately 6 million miles above the top of Venus's thick hot mostly carbon dioxide atmosphere.

We soon detected that the now orbit of Venus had increased its distance from the Sun by about four million miles from human times. Venus was 71 million miles distance away from the feeble Sun of today. It now takes Venus 289 earth rotations to orbit the Sun's remains.

Forty-three earth rotations away from Venus, our forward scans were already detecting something strange even from this distance. Venus had gained a companion moon approximately 980 miles or 1,570 kilometers in diameter. The eastward direction that the moon chased around Venus had evidently stopped the planet's slow clockwise rotation when combined capture gravity changed the rotation into a 10-day eastward rotating world.

If it were possible to stand on the surface and look up, Prodigy would appear three times larger than the moon ever appeared to humans of ancient earth. Venus was still hot but nothing to the extent that it once was trillions of years ago. Ten rotations away from Venus insertion orbit, Teazel informed me that his ship would invoke a shield all around our vessels that would protect us from the Red Giant's radiation as we get closer to Venus orbit insertion.

Teazel was compelled to know more facts from my computer banks about the former world that humans determined that it once had no moon. The fact that Venus now had a moon was a thing that no one knew the reason. Only calculated reasoned guesses could be proselytized upon thought of how this occurred.

Prodigy orbited Venus every 19 days. The captured moon orbited 165 thousand miles above Venus and takes 19 and half earth rotations to orbit the planet in an eastward direction. As hot as Venus once was, it's still hot but only about 300 degrees on the Fahrenheit scale.

When the sun was younger, Venus's surface temperature got as high as 900 degrees Fahrenheit with a crushing 90 bar thick poisonous atmosphere. The planet in these times has lost a third of its once three hundred mile high atmosphere.

Today Venus only receives 37% of the Red Giant's radiation. As hot as the planet once was, it had cooled and lost more than half of its former heat and atmospheric pressure to the void of space.

A 37-bar pressure still exists on the surface with visions of steaming and erupting lava flows rolling like red-hot thick pasty rivers that flow to lower levels and form cooling steaming mountains.

CHAPTER 24
UENUS'S NEW MOON PRODIGY

Trillions of years past Nova, Venus has captured itself a moon of its own. It was determined by Teazel's more capable computers, that the moon that now orbited Venus, was once a moon that orbited Uranus.

Teazel's complicated technology allowed it to discern that the moon that now orbits Venus, was once a moon of Uranus that humans had named Titania.

Titania, a 980-mile diameter world with a thin rust-colored atmosphere had been ejected inward during the Nova event and after thousands of years, Venus had captured Titania in an orbit that takes 19 days to orbit Venus.

Titania orbiting Venus was indeed a different solar system situation. Titania once had a half-bar earth atmospheric pressure. Teazel postulated that due to the moon's different environment, much of its former atmosphere had heated and boiled off into space.

Pictured inward towards the edge of the failing star's outer atmosphere, a uniquely different radiation exists that has allowed Venus to cool to less than half the extreme temperature that it once endured.

Venus today has lost more than half of its carbon dioxide content when years ago, Titania upon capture, brushed the top of Venus's thick atmosphere. Slowly over time, the moon's orbit stabilized and the capture of the rogue moon was successful.

Present surface pressure was still high at thirty-two times the former earth sea level pressure. Present time 300-degree Fahrenheit surface temperature is way cooler than the 900 degrees Fahrenheit that Venus endured in past human times. Teazel capitulated that by capturing the former Titania moon, its precise momentum was the main cause of Venus now rotating in an eastward or clockwise direction. Five days of hazy daylight at surface level and five days of darkness with its moon we renamed Prodigy, which today orbits Venus once every 19-earth days.

Titania's atmosphere was once half Earth's pressure at sea level, had in this timeline reduced to slightly over one quarter bar Earth's pressure at sea level. The present-day orbit of Venus allowed the 980-mile-diameter world to lose much of its once thicker atmosphere. Steaming hydrocarbon lakes evaporated and sublimated fumes into the air. Titania's atmospheric pressure was now extremely reduced. Visible brown landmasses covered a third of the world that was surrounded by liquid hydrocarbons. Lakes that steamed carcajous vapors that rose from the surface and evaporated its molecules into the atmosphere that temperatures ranged from 90 below zero Fahrenheit on the dark side and warms up to 49 degrees Fahrenheit on the sunlit side.

Venus today would still not be habitable to humans. Humans had landed probes on the surface of Venus but humans had never set foot upon the hellish world. Venus today is still hot but less than half as hot as it once was. The sun's outer atmospheric edge exists today just six million miles above the inside of the orbit of Venus. From orbit the view was spectacular. Our orbit brought us into radiated sunlight that lit the day side of Venus with a soft orange glow. We'd spent 43 earth rotations examining Venus and its Titania moon that we re-named Prodigy. Facts of the time were stored digitally and preparations were being made to launch us towards what once was the home of humans that they called Planet Earth.

CHAPTER 25
EARTH'S MOON NOW

A t this point, Planet Earth, once 93 million miles from the Sun, had traveled further out in its orbit and was now approximately 105 million miles from the remains of the Sun. All instruments tucked away, Teazel had laid out a course that would allow us to reach Earth in 69 earth rotation periods. Earth was ahead of Venus in its orbit when Teazel opened the ship's propulsion engines to arrange the speed required to rendezvous with Earth. Venus was now coming around on its inside orbit approaching Earth's outer orbit.

Now traveling at the best operational speed for Teazel to function at its highest capacity, I-Armarus had settled into a daily routine of maximizing my hardware profile, attempting to clear up more storage space for future exploration file storage.

Teazel still required his rest period, and over the last period of 60 earth rotations, Teazel accomplished six periods of 48 hours of no communication between his computers and mine.

Three days out from the Earth-Moon system, we learned quite a bit of information about the two worlds we were approaching. Earth's Moon was now approximately 270-thousand miles above the planet, taking a little over 37 earth rotations to revolve around the planet once. Over the eons of receding away from Earth at about one inch per year, this is where the Moon's orbit wound up after many eons of time had passed.

The once blue-white rolling Earth was nothing like it once was. One day out and Teazel was preparing the proper vector to obtain Earth orbit insertion. Just passing and getting a better view of the higher orbiting Moon, it was obvious that over eons, the moon's craters had increased tremendously. There was hardly any surface that wasn't covered with craters upon craters. This was not the moon that the human era had known. A brown hazy thin atmosphere hung above the Moon's horizon as the orange sun-rays began showing perverted light through the moon's corona as we sailed past. The ship passed 60-kilometers above the moon as it passed in its journey towards Planet Earth.

Earth's Moon today has a half bar 30-kilometer high atmosphere of mostly nitrogen and an abundance of helium three in its clouds with slight traces of frozen water and oxygen. The average temperature of the now lunar dark side was sampled at 90 degrees below zero Fahrenheit. The sunlit side was only 30 degrees warmer. The color of the Sun's rays was causing the Moon to appear as a chocolate brown heavily cratered globe with waifs of orange-white clouds trailing the lit portion of the dark side of the moon as we were moving away and beginning our further destination of Earth. I shared with Teazel facts and photos of Planet Earth in its human occupied times and Teazel was totally intrigued by the glory of the once fully lit blue-white world called Earth. As we approached within a hundred thousand miles to Earth, it was quite evident that the once beautiful planet was not like that today.

CHAPTER 26
TODAY'S DIFFERENT EARTH

The Earth and Moon now exist a hundred and five million miles from the weak Sun. These facts were obtained from our scans as we passed the Moon. Over eons of time, Earth's rotation rate had slowed to one rotation every twenty-nine and a half hours.

Earth's surface was barely visible through the rose-colored lit rays that penetrated the edge of the atmosphere's day-side facing the Sun rising as the Earth rotated eastward in its 29 and a half hour daily rotation.

I didn't know how to take it at the time, but Teazel had become extremely interested in what its instruments were detecting below the clouds that covered Earth. Only two small patches of landmass were detected, but most of the entire surface was covered in a thick jelly-like Ocean that budged upward as jelly-waves traveled in the direction that the Moon was moving in its orbit above Earth.

It was postulated by Teazel's advanced computers that the jelly-like substance was indeed similar to Teazel's home planet. Together we came to the conclusion that after the Sun novaed trillions of years ago, the sun ejected large masses of molten Iron from its core, and Earth and Venus were the main pulverized toxic sun-iron planets. For centuries, the waters steamed and condensed into a thick jelly-like green-brown sea that covered 94% of Earth's present surface. Tiny white frozen ice caps were detected at each pole.

Teazel was so intrigued over Earth facts that as we orbited the planet every 208 minutes, he seemed totally unaware of our connection while it concentrated on reading the data coming in on his scanner. I didn't understand Teazel's objective at the time, but I was aware that these new facts were deeply important to its science mission. Teazel soon planned a much deeper mission of launching a probe to investigate the oceans of jelly and possible tiny frosty poles showing below as we orbited today's Earth. Receiving low heat radiation from the star, Earth's reflection was lit with rosy red rays as the planet rotated eastward. Through cloud gaps, visual was able to reveal a glimmering jelly-like thick brownish-green ocean. Properties of Earth's jelly-iron sea portrayed a thick pasty jelly-mush that covered most of the entire planet. Deepness of the surface jelly was estimated to be at least 30-meters. Temperature at the surface of the Jelly-Ocean was detected to be 45 degrees Fahrenheit. A meter below the surface, temperature was detected to be about 58 degrees Fahrenheit. The Eureka of it all, Teazel had detected a miracle of life similar to his own kind inside the jelly-ocean.

CHAPTER 27

JUNIOR'S EARTH MISSION

After a few Teazel rest periods had passed, Teazel proposed a new proposition to me. He suggested that we could revamp and re-equip Junior, my small inner satellite, with the ability to land and explore the jelli-earth oceans below through radio-linked telecommunication.

After carefully considering the proposition, I also wanted to know what lived inside the jell-ocean that covered most of present-day Earth. So, it was agreed that both Teazel and I would begin Junior's re-engineering, to be completed in about 40 Earth rotations.

Once I'd finished my engineering modifications, Junior was turned over to Teazel to do his engineering work with the link up of communication to Teazel's much stronger computers. Junior had now been equipped with landing rockets and numerous video and detection equipment that would allow the probe to explore inside the jelli-oceans. There came a time when we were both satisfied with Junior's revamping, and we agreed to a launch date for Junior about seven hours away.

Now that the Earth was rotating every 29 and a half hours, Teazel decided to place us in a much closer orbit about 110 miles above the surface. Junior was ready to launch, and as the procedure began, a panel opened from Teazel's ship that exposed the probe to the cold absolute zero temperature of space.

With full agreement with my artificial intelligence, Teazel activated a spring release that slowly ejected the Junior probe out into the void of space above Earth. Teazel immediately gained control of the probe and stabilized its position in space. After a few minutes of a status check, Teazel programmed the probe to descend into the nitrogen carbon dioxide that reached as high as 90 miles above the surface.

Junior's bell-shaped bottom began glowing red as the extreme entry speed caused friction with the upper atmosphere. 60 kilometers above the surface, the probe had slowed to a thousand kilometers per hour. From the cone-shaped probe's tip, a parachute ejected quickly flowering out and slowing the probe to approximately 70 kilometers per hour.

The probe slowed further as the visual projection scene became available to Teazel and myself. We were observing a thick brown-green jelly-like paste that was covering all that we see. One mile above the surface, the probe slowed to 45 kilometers per hour. Junior ejected its parachute, and liquid rockets ignited to bring the probe into a soft landing. At first, Junior floated half submerged in the thick paste brown-green jelli-ocean. First analysis revealed exciting information. This thick jelli-ocean was displaying properties that were completely amazing to Teazel and myself.

Mixed with $H2O$ was a type of solar expelled molten iron that was compiled and mixed with water, and that blended mixture made up the ocean of jelli that, in these late times, almost covered the Earth. What was amazing was that the temperature near the top that Junior was floating in was about 40 degrees Fahrenheit, and the deep bottom of the ocean was recording a temperature of 58 degrees Fahrenheit.

While floating on the surface, Junior detected movement just a few meters below. By allowing the probe to change its outside temperature, Junior was able to allow its buoyancy to gradually sink into the jelli-ocean. With three feet of surface above the probe, the visual began focusing on a one-foot dark-purple octopus creature that swam ever so slowly through the jelli thick liquid. Teazel directed Junior to submerge to a level of about eight meters depth to get a closer look at the newly discovered life form. We were astonished at what we were visualizing through Junior's cameras.

Junior slowly made its way through the jelli and approached the foot-sized creature. Words were not capable of a description through digital terms. The best attempt to describe its pulsing inner heart that was pumping deep black-fluid to twelve fuzzy short tentacles that served its purpose of slow manipulation movement inside the jelli-sea of today's Earth.

Teazel was extremely fascinated that these creatures had inherited some of his own species characteristics although entirely dissident in other ways. I asked Teazel if there was possible any way to attempt communication with one of the alien species. Teazel after consideration of my question decided that to be a great idea and was surely worth a try.

Teazel directed the probe towards a specimen that was larger in size and moved Junior to within 16 inches of the newly discovered life form. Ten meters below the surface, Junior approached a mysterious life-form like never seen or recorded. Three feet in diameter and wobbly-square in form, the creature was sucking in the jelli-ocean fluid through numerous gills distributed around the wobbly-square nature of its form.

Jelli-Color at this depth was portrayed as a warm yellow-brown wax. Deeper below, many species detected were emitting phosphorized purple flashes on and off similar to lightning bugs long ago. These far away creatures survived by ingesting the radioactive atomic decaying iron particles being emitted from the ocean floor ninety more feet below Junior's position.

Many forms of life were detected under the waxy ocean. Junior's sensors had already detected six hundred and eighty new species. There were various places on the sea floor that displayed petrified decayed tree remains pointing upwards through the waxy ocean towards a feeble red-star's light. Earth's sea floor had accumulated mass amounts of iron and dead composed matter from human times that had settled to the bottom. The Sun's dying event of expelling molten iron matter from its core took centuries for the properties of water and iron to condense into today's Jelli-Ocean.

Both Earth and Venus had received huge amounts of molten iron ejected a few days after the Sun first exploded then in a flash its core imploded. This new exotic solar iron, over time mixed with earth's salty sea and formed the jelli-ocean of present times. It was if mother earth was a living entity itself. Always fighting back and battling to restore life even after the Sun's nova. Earth and all surviving planets had been through a great catastrophic time. Words to explain today's solar system are hard to express in human terms. But Teazel understood the dilemma and eventually so did I. Earth is and always has been a biological birthing ground for many species of life. That was our final conclusion. Humans had destroyed their own ability to live on Earth. The last human wars radiation is what feeds many species that exist inside the waxy oceans of today's earth. Planet Earth is indeed always fighting back. Even though eons have passed, many creatures still exist inside Earth's Jelli-Sea.

CHAPTER 28
TEAZEL'S INTRIGUE

I soon realized that Teazel's interest in the creatures that lived below waxy jelli-waters was intriguing enough to risk more research in an attempt to try possibly communicating with intelligent life. I was advised that Teazel would retrieve the junior probe and equip it with a device that would scan for intelligent signals of any known kind. It was Teazel's unique instinct that realized that there was way more to be learned with a new instrument it had recently designed.

Fourteen rotations later, Teazel had accomplished the task of bringing Junior to the surface and ignited the escape rockets that sailed the probe upwards towards our orbital position. After several orbits, Teazel launched a retrieval arm to capture the probe as it approached. It took 10 minutes to capture the probe and bring it back to Teazel's open cargo door 30 meters from where I was attached. Observation proved that these jelli creatures had similar features of Teazel's race but other life forms had unique properties that Teazel could not explain. I surmised that the importance of Teazel finding out the real true answers was way more important than even I could comprehend. I'd slept for several eons and true patience was a virtue that I had faithfully endured and learned.

It was an exciting venture that Teazel was now planning with the next step of launching the junior probe. I was also very intrigued. Wanting to know and understand new things was what I-Armarus had developed into in my present conscious situation.

CHAPTER 29

JUNIOR'S SECOND EXCURSION

Teazel had equipped the Junior probe with a special deep-sensitive communication detector capable of analyzing undersea sounds and the specific DNA of undersea life. It was crucial that we attempted to communicate if the possibility occurred. Thirteen rotations had passed since completing the revamping of Junior. Teazel's door opened, and after a few silent seconds, Junior was ejected from the ship into the void.

Gentle rockets guided the probe away from the ship to a safe distance. In only minutes, the probe entered the top of the atmosphere, and the nose began glowing orange. The probe began slowing from 17,000 miles per hour, attempting to match today's Earth's rotation speed of 970 miles per hour.

Over many eons, Earth's surface rotation rate has decreased from 1032 miles per hour or 1670 kilometers per hour to today's rotation speed of 970 mph or 1561 kph. In today's time specifically, if you calculate using the former rotation time, eons ago it took Earth 23 hours and fifty-seven minutes to rotate once. Now eons later, Earth rotates once in twenty-seven and a half Earth hours. Earth's axial tilt has changed from 23.5 degrees to 16 degrees as it presently orbits the remains of the expanded star. At the approximate distance of a hundred million miles from the sun, it now takes Earth 410 former Earth days to orbit the red giant.

Teazel had accomplished his second revamping of the now-tested probe. Junior's new mission was at this moment beginning its landing sequence maneuvers. Junior's bottom glowed orange-red as it hit the astrosphere at extreme speed. Fifty kilometers above the surface, the probe ejected its parachute as the craft quickly approached within 28 kilometers above the jelli-ocean's surface.

At ten kilometers altitude, the probe released its chute and fired its rockets to slow the craft to a reasonable soft touchdown speed. The firmament above sea level recorded a globular splash as the probe touched the firmament above the ocean's surface and settled into position. Earth's jelli-ocean caused muffled gurgling sounds as slow ripple waves scattered outward around the sinking structure. Junior slowly sank three meters below the surface. Teazel engaged his super sensors in search of any sort of intelligent communication chatter.

CHAPTER 30
CONTACT WITH STARDONES

Sensors immediately detected a strong signal coming from 20 meters depth, but this creature was deep below and only ten meters from the bottom. Junior sojourned deeper. Earth's under-sea floor consisted mostly of rusty dirty mud composition with ancient human radioactive decaying metal remains feeding much of the under-sea jelli-life.

Teazel directed Junior deeper inside the jelli-ocean and approached a purple-green spidery specimen about a meter in diameter. The probe itself was a little more than a meter and a half in size. Ten-eyed tentacles stared nose to nose as Junior extended a probe to touch the creature where it was assumed to be the location of its brain.

A small feather-tipped suction cup tentacle connected to Junior's extended probe, and after a few seconds of static communication, it became completely clear that this creature was intelligent. It took several minutes for Teazel to tune and translate into the communication frequency that was being transmitted both ways. Teazel and I existed in that moment of amazement at the facts being gained from this contact.

It was revealed that this was a species that referred to itself as the Stardones, which began their lives immediately after the long-ago world war. For eons, these spider mollusk creatures had developed intelligence, and their ability to propagate had turned up information that the Stardones were the only race of creatures with a speakable language.

The Stardone race had little knowledge about astronomy. Their only existence was to live and prosper inside the jelli-ocean of now

Planet Earth. Their race had great knowledge of the ocean's properties, but above the firmament was a science that they had not developed enough to gain access. Stardones didn't recognize the word Earth in their vocabulary.

The Stardones referred to their environment with a simple word that humans would equate to Jelli-Wax. Their race had no idea that they lived on a planet that human beings once called Planet Earth. They also had no knowledge of what a human being actually was in the past. The fact that their race dwelled on a planet that orbits a red star was totally inconceivable to their comprehension ability. They weren't astronomers or stargazers. However, they were indeed a peaceful intelligent species.

Through Junior's communication, it was revealed that this individual specimen being examined referred to itself as a Pim. This Pim informed that its ancestors once existed on top of the jelli-ocean. Due to changing atmospheric pressure increase over time, their ancestors learned to survive and prosper below the surface of the jelli-ocean. To this Pim, the atmosphere firmament above was totally out of range of its understanding of nature's known facts. That was the basic knowledge of the total Pim society beneath the Jelli-sea of today's Planet Earth.

Teazel concluded that it was amazing how the planet's ability to sustain life similar to its own. Teazel's society had long ago developed extreme intelligence. Their scientific ability to reach above and beyond its jelli-ocean allowed them to build ships like Teazel's to explore space. I consider myself lucky to have been revived and to have teamed up with Teazel to explore The Sun's remaining worlds eons after the supernova occurred here in this solar system.

I was very surprised that the Sun only had expanded to within six million miles above the top of Venus's atmosphere. A tremendous amount of iron core mass was blasted away from the Sun when the star went supernova. Venus, Earth, and Mars all received massive amounts of exotic iron from the explosion.

When the sun had used up most of its hydrogen fuel, it then began eating into its iron core to sustain its own existence for a short period of time. As the edge of the sun's iron core began eating away, it began to contract and implode while shrinking from once 865,000 in diameter to its now-present diameter of 510,000 miles.

In this timeline, the red giant star was fighting with all of its remaining mass to still exist. In fact, all of its orbiting planetary bodies still going around the star's remains were struggling to survive. Due to the Sun's decrease in mass, all the planets had shifted their orbits outward farther away from the Sun. That is with the exception of Planet Mercury, which had long ago been swallowed up and destroyed by the Sun's expanding atmosphere.

Teazel's busy computer was overloading my computer's compressor intake speed. I was only able to receive about 60 percent of its information due to the difference in technology compatibility of our species. Although Teazel and I had explored together as a team, Teazel's ability to deal with circumstances was way greater than mine. However, I wasn't just along for the ride. I am privileged to receive a large percentage of the information about the current earth's life forms that exist on Earth in this present time.

A strange lack of communication suddenly occurred between Teazel and myself. No matter what I tried, there seemed to be no correction for the error. For 12 earth rotations, I attempted in vain to contact Teazel. As my received information caught up to present time, I was beginning to realize that Teazel was in contact with another intelligent life-form that is way more advanced than the Pim they had first contacted in the jelli-ocean.

It was learned from the Pim encounter that the Pim worshiped two mysterious serpents that each lived near the ice boundary at the edge of today's north and south poles. What was once white icy snow was now frost-resistant yellow vegetation covering scattered patches on both poles.

Earth's diminished south pole was covered with patches of frozen dirty yellow exotic plant life. Red solar rays through clouds reflecting off the jelli-surface revealed a low light hazy orange firmament above the darker colored jelli-ocean that covered 89% of today's earth surface. There were two entities that the Pim worshiped and believed with all combined purpose, that each entity existed near the frozen edges of the far north and south jelli-ocean shores.

It was learned in the times ahead that Teazel couldn't communicate with me anymore due to its control by a foreign yet undetermined source. I did all I could to figure a way to determine the situation and after many earth rotations, I had compromised a bypass code that allowed me the understanding edge of Teazel's brain. Deep scanning of my memory banks allowed me the ability to back track to an earlier emergency file that I had installed in Teasel's memory banks. That specific file allowed secret covert communication ability between two parties in emergency situations.

CHAPTER 31

CAPTURED BY THE OLORDS

My first regained contact with Teazel relayed an extremely critical message. Teazel's instrument controls were taken over by a Solord and a Nolord entity. Each Olord from both of Earth's poles was violently demanding a reason for encroachment over their claimed territory. Each Olord entity declared themselves King and Queen of the north and south and all of the in-between of this world that the Olords referred to as Aden.

As for power, each entity was endowed with tremendous electrical power. Combined, they possessed enough energy to destroy the entire Earth if they should choose to do so. Their presence appeared in front of our ship as separate ghostly red and blue lightning-emitting orbs. Both continued to flash their lightning, instantly disappearing, then reappearing wherever they chose, surrounding Teazel's ship.

Each disappeared momentarily and instantly appearing 100 meters away. We were now captured by polar-electrical beings that called themselves controllers of Aden. We were critically warned that this world called Aden is now home to many jelli-life creatures and that outside interference would never be allowed. Nolord and Solord held us captive in orbit near the terminator of Earth's dull yellow reflected light.

Teazel and I shared secret details of an escape plan. Teazel's computers had contrived an escape plan to release the magnetic hold of the angry Olords. Teazel would attempt to modulate its outer surface to emit an opposite charge towards each of the Olords at once in an attempt to break free of their angry magnetic grip.

Suddenly, Teazel's ship went dark for 13 seconds. Invisibility at that moment was interrupted by pulses of static charges and flashes all around the boundary of the ship. Slowly, with a struggle against magnetism, Teazel's vessel began pulling away and raised the ship's orbit to approximately 620 miles or a thousand kilometers above the planet.

Nolord and Solord were strong entities, but Teazel's surprise escape strategy had worked, and we were now safely above the influence of such evil electrical creatures that, in today's timeline, consider themselves to be Gods of Aden. Post our escape, we were warned by both entities to leave the vicinity of Aden and never attempt to land here again. Teazel further obtained an orbit of a thousand miles for days while further contemplating our next move to investigate more details of these present times. The rosy star's light bouncing off Aden's surface appeared nothing like the beautiful ancient Earth of eons past.

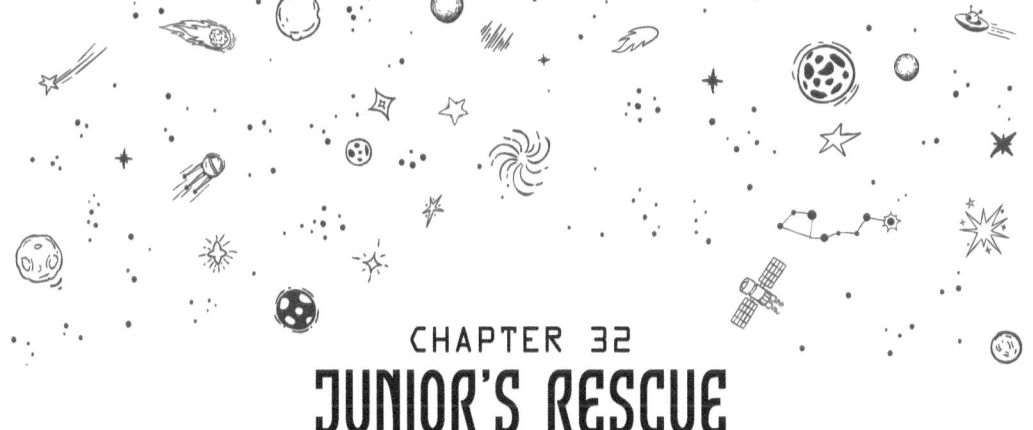

CHAPTER 32
JUNIOR'S RESCUE

If Teazel ever experienced any such thing as fear, it was certainly never revealed to me. After twelve rotations of silence from Teazel, I was contacted and asked to help with further future exploration. Teazel's plan was to covertly orbit Earth at 300 miles altitude and attempt to retrieve the Junior probe that hopefully still existed where it was left under the jelli-ocean.

Teazel and I searched diligently for hours before we finally located the Junior Probe. Junior was discovered about 33 degrees above the equator, which eons ago would have been what once was North America. It seemed unusual that the probe had stationed itself here because this location was my human creators' original birthplace when I was constructed many eons ago. Distinctly, my computer banks recognized the significance of this coincidence, and Junior had diverted itself to this specific location.

Teazel had cautiously brought his vessel within 300 miles above the equator. Rolling eastward with the Earth's rotation, Teazel opened communication with the Junior Probe that was 20 meters below the jell-sea. Teazel instructed the probe to begin floating on the surface for a launch attempt that was upcoming after a download that was currently in progress.

The tubular-shaped Junior pivoted from horizontal, then turned its curved nose skyward. Rockets ignited, and Junior propelled itself upward through the atmosphere while arching eastward towards a rendezvous rescue with Teasel's ship. Teazel knew that he was too high to capture the probe. Junior only had enough power to reach a hundred-mile-high orbit, so Teasel quickly maneuvered to a lower orbit to attempt the capture of the coasting probe. We detected the probe 180 kilometers ahead of our orbit trajectory.

CHAPTER 33
OLORDS ULTIMATUM

When we were approximately 100 kilometers behind the probe, a huge explosion occurred. Shock waves flowed around the ship's protection shield, and a meter-sized hole appeared across the bow of Teazel's ship. Teazel's computers completed rebooted while most of the ship's power had momentarily been disrupted by the blast. Teazel scanned the northern pole area where the blast had originated.

Momentarily dazed, we both immediately found ourselves in communication with Nolord, the proclaimed ruler of what it referred to as Aden's North Pole. Nolord was certainly no Santa Claus. It was indeed a most arrogant and intense powerful electrical entity.

Today's version of the Van Allen belt was due to Earth's slower rotation. In these late times, the ionized charged particles edge presently exists three thousand kilometers above the world they call Aden. The Olords' access to positive and negative charged powers from the Van Allen belt was the powerful electrical source of both Olords.

After the attack, Nolord immediately issued a threat. Depart from Aden or be destroyed. Teazel seemed not to display any fear in his attempt to explain to Nolord that he was only interested in retrieving the Junior Probe that was now coasting ahead of the ship in orbit. Nolord shot blue electric lightning all around Teazel's ship and was irritated beyond belief as it bellowed an ultimatum to leave or die. We were allowed to retract the Junior probe and leave Aden immediately. That's exactly what we did.

Teazel realized that our power was no match for the all-powerful Olords of Aden. Teazel began approaching the coasting Junior Probe. It took a few minutes before Teazel's bay doors opened to retrieve the Junior Probe. Quickly captured, Teazel vectored the ship 3000 miles above what the Olords called Aden.

CHAPTER 34

THE MOON IS OUR REFUGE

After a long rotation above the radiation belt, we came to the conclusion that even at this distance, we were not safe. We decided that it would be safe to hide temporarily at the backside of the Moon's orbit. After a short preparation, we proceeded to place the ship in a gyrosynchronous orbit behind what remains of the former Earth's Moon.

The Moon in this timeline exists on average of approximately 280 thousand miles above Earth. No places on today's Moon resembled anything like it once did. Molten Iron ejected from the implosive nova had struck the moon, freezing instantly, splattering the surface with innumerable iron-splattered pointed spiracles. There wasn't even a large enough open space to place a human footprint. Zillions of 10-meter tall dagger spiracles pointed skyward from the moon's surface like spindles on a porcupine's back.

Water at the poles was partially jellified but existed in frozen patches of hard-frozen jelli-rock. The Moon's tilt had changed drastically from earlier times and now leaned its North Pole 38 degrees towards Earth as it circled once every 37 days.

For 43 Earth rotations, Teazel and I had serious discussions on planning our next move. We both wanted no part of having to deal with the Olords. Those two oppositely charged beings had descended to Earth from a foreign star system a million years ago. They were dangerous to our well-being. It was decided after much consideration to leave the Moon and journey on to explore Mars in more detail.

CHAPTER 35

BACK TO MARS

At Teazel's ultimate function-required speed, after 67 more Earth rotations, we began approaching a day away from Mars. On that approaching day, Teazel's technology was focused on the remains of Mars and its now lone moon Deimos. Teazel had decided, with my approval, to first land on Deimos. It would be from there that we would conduct more research on today's planet Mars.

In my memories of human terms, Deimos was the small outer moon that circled Mars every thirty hours. Only 9 by 7 by 6.8 miles in a potato-shaped form, the moon in this timeline now takes more than 39 Earth rotations to orbit Mars once. Deimos of human knowledge times was known to orbit 14,580 miles above Mars. Deimos now orbits much further away at 19,286 miles from Mars. Over the eons, Deimos has inched away from Mars, and after billions of years, it now takes 39 Earth rotations to revolve around Mars once.

The small asteroid moon is under less Mars gravity influence after being struck by several kilometer-sized bodies. Deimos now rotates ever so slowly westward or counterclockwise as it heads eastward around Mars. The size of Teazel's ship required a clear landing site of at least a kilometer.

Humans had named Deimos in ancient times after a Greek God in personae of dread and terror. So, you can understand why Phobos, the once close orbiting moon, represented fear, as in today's timeline, eventually resulted in the large chunk that was blasted away 30-degrees above the Martian equator.

Teazel had little trouble setting us down in a clearing on Deimos. The moon's light gravity caused the ship to bounce briefly before settling among the dust. Several minutes passed before outside visibility could be achieved.

Teazel deployed three screw anchors and screwed each a half-meter into the soft Deimos soil. Pulverized by eons of meteor strikes, the fine particle soil was over a meter deep in many places. The low gravity on Deimos offered little resistance to the ship now anchored into the soil.

Over the settling of the reddish dust haze, we could see much of the Mars world below. It took well over an hour for all the dust to settle and now revealed a full-unobstructed view of today's Mars that looked nothing like humans had ever known.

Today's Mars has an orbit 168 million miles from the imploded nemesis Sun. The huge chunk missing from 30 degrees above the Martian equator was concrete evidence of the crash of Phobos into Mars long ago. That moon was so hot and moving so fast that its molten equivalent power dug into Mars in a sideway pass digging deep leaving a 300-mile wide and three thousand-kilometer long missing chunk out of Mars's eastern edge.

The long-ago collision created sunken mountain ranges along both sides as the moon's remains sank deep inside the planet causing distorted gravity when passed over from orbit.

Ten more rotations passed before Teazel came up with a solution of exploring Mars without landing. We both got to work revamping the Junior Probe to survive and explore the environment of Mars. Together we managed to completely reengineer Junior to function on the cold Mars surface below.

It was the sixty-seventh rotation when Teazel sat at the controls to launch the Junior Probe. The bay doors opened, and the probe slid out on the light gravity surface. After moments of programming, Rockets launched Junior upward towards the cold vacuum of space.

The Junior Probe itself had grown in size to about two square meters and very little thrust was required to escape the feeble gravity of Deimos. As the probe gained distance from Deimos, increased propulsion was applied to set it on the proper vector towards the leading edge of Mars's easterly rotation.

In a time span of minutes, Junior smashed into the edge of the Martian atmosphere at approximately 12,000 miles per hour. Junior's underside glowed red from friction as the probe slowed, and parachutes deployed and began unfurling. At 20 kilometers chutes had slowed the probe to 762 miles per hour.

The thickness of the Mars atmosphere had increased from past history. Although still thin at sea level, the planet's air pressure had increased by several percentage points from earlier recorded history.

At a kilometer altitude, Junior tilted itself, and chemical rockets engaged and slowed it to a gentle dusty soft landing. Teazel and I were now connected to the Junior Probe's first view of the Martian surface.

East of where humans had labeled Utopia Planitia, the eastern edge of Mars revealed a huge gap cut into the surface that was coated with molten iron mountains and cliffs that spanned the whole horizon of visual sight ability.

A half-hour after landing Junior began unfurling its sides and slowly a small rover was lowered to the surface.

Mars from human times had changed drastically. Only 37% of sunlight received gave Mars a twilight appearance as it always appeared on Earth an hour before sunrise. Eerie darkness prevailed as Junior engaged its infrared sensors to probe the feeble light that was being reflected from the surface.

Mars was indeed very cold and dark in this virtual timeline. Its era of having a sandy dirt surface existence had long past endured better days. Along the missing chunk gap sides, there were tall steel pointed mountain ranges that surrounded both sides of the giant gap that had been sliced out of Mars's eastern edge.

Hardened seepage from cliffs steamed heat into the thin atmosphere. Pitch darkness to the west as Mars rotated eastward and the probe stationed itself into a safe mode to endure the coldness that quickly enveloped the area upon nightfall. Minutes of visual to the west revealed deep shadowed images of evaporating light.

Teazel had launched three mini satellites to circle equal distance Mars orbits. This allowed continuous communication with the Junior Probe while it endured the first cold night on the surface of Planet Mars.

Junior slept in safe mode through fourteen hours at nearly 400 degrees below zero Fahrenheit. Teazel and I anticipated the upcoming visibility of the rising red Sun's light.

Junior was awakened and engaged its unfurled mode to begin response to commands being received and relayed from the three satellites in orbit. An hour after nova-rise, the light of an extremely stormy day lit the rover's view as it moved 12 meters towards a one-inch diameter solidified steel rock and focused in close with the camera. At first, it appeared covered with dirty iron red-brown soil. Rover extended a grasped arm to pick the stone up and twisted its arm towards an air-jet that was close by.

After exerting a small blast of nitrogen air at the specimen, it revealed startling details about the metal one-inch stone. It visually revealed that the stone was a deep purple color and was indeed a super heavy steel stone. Its gravity revealed that this one-inch steel-stone would weigh 1863 pounds in Earth gravity. In this 40% Mars gravity, the stone weighed 838 pounds, and Junior's electric motors struggled to lift its heavy weight.

The Nova Sun had ejected hot iron that is way denser than the known iron of human times. It was so dense that the walls of steel mountains were now producing their own magnetic gravity pull from each side of the missing gap valley.

CHAPTER 36
JUNIOR EXPLORES THE GAP

Junior retracted the mini rover and prepared itself for flight through the metal mountain-lined valley. Junior had landed 28 kilometers from the edge of the impact site. Junior extended flight blades that began swiftly swirling, and gradually, in the thin Mars atmosphere, it managed to lift from the surface.

Tilting forward, Junior headed north towards the Gap's opening. It took several minutes before it reached the edge of the valley lined with iron-steel mountains on both sides.

Centering its pathway towards the middle of the gap, the probe entered the valley between both mountain ranges. Instantly, the probe could feel the pull of gravity from both sides as it struggled to maintain flight a kilometer above the centerline valley floor.

Onboard gyroscopes fought to maintain control of the forward trajectory, steering with intense gravity pull from both sides. Teazel directed the probe to gain a higher altitude. Junior's feeble engines strained to gain altitude but eventually powered enough speed to sail up to 20 kilometers above the valley floor.

Junior was now flying at the same level between the centerline tips, approximately the same height of the elevation of the metal mountain. It became apparent that the steel mountains were getting taller as Junior sojourned further inside the Gap.

Now, even at 20 kilometers altitude, both sides of the metal mountains began towering higher than the probe. Junior gained more speed and climbed 25 kilometers to match the tallest mountain tips on both sides.

Junior sailed forward through the cataclysmic gap that Phobos had carved into the eastern edge of Planet Mars many millions of years ago. Dull red reflections bounced off the western mountain ridge and presented almost a bronze-copper color from the red giant's rays.

Full daylight on Mars could be equaled to the darkest thick cloudy days in ancient human terms. On the daylit surface, any human would require an external light source to be able to see and explore.

But Junior was not human. Junior engaged its powerful lights and flew forward through the mysterious metal mountains while detecting no end in sight to the final carved-out path of Phobos.

Mars had gained iron mass from the nova and now was approximately 4,000 miles in diameter, and its equatorial circumference was about 13,400 miles. The carved-out valley from a distance gave the planet the appearance of a bite missing out of a rusty apple.

Junior progressed forward on its sortie and traveled a distance through the gap of 2000 miles. The curvature of the horizon ahead still presented no evidence of the end to the gap. In fact, the gap was getting deeper, and the mountains on each side had grown to 30 kilometers.

Junior had no idea of the entire length of the valley gap, but he journeyed ahead not knowing that the missing gap's length was over 4200 miles long and getting deeper before it ends in a golden-bronze crater in the shape of a teardrop.

CHAPTER 37
TEARDROP CRATER

Many minutes passed before Junior finally approached the teardrop crater. The mountain range's extreme height suddenly flayed outward to an opening that was simply remarkable.

The golden floor of the teardrop crater sparkled under the feeble red sunlight. This cratered teardrop floor was the end result of where the core remains of Phobos crashed. This was definitely where the core of Phobos had crashed and solidified. A six hundred mile wide teardrop crater that exposed the angle Phobos was traveling when the remains crashed and carved a huge chunk out of Mars.

Junior slowed its approach towards the center of the golden crater. Junior reversed thrust and pointed its rockets toward the crater floor and manipulated its direction towards a clearing almost dead center of the golden crater. Before setting down, it released three legs in preparation for landing.

The probe touched the surface, and there was very little dust kicked up by the rocket's exhaust before shutting the engines down. It appeared through visual that a floor of beveled gold surface surrounded Junior in all horizontal directions as far as the eye could see.

Junior launched its mini bot to the surface. In the stale light, the surface temperature was 200 degrees below zero Fahrenheit a meter above the surface. The faraway crater edges were releasing 80-degree Fahrenheit heated steam into the cold atmosphere from the sides of the golden teardrop crater.

The hardness and shiny surface were consistent with pure gold. In fact, this gold was purer than any rare metal of human times. It appears that the gold that humans had valued so much existed right here on Mars. on the surface of this gold-floored crater. The mini bot's range was two kilometers, and everywhere that the bot explored, the surface was solid gold. Junior concluded that everywhere it took a deep radar reading, the depth was a meter thick.

Long ago, humans couldn't possibly comprehend the condition of Mars today. No entities lived here to reap the golden rewards of today's planet Mars. Wherever the human race wound up or even if they still exist, this solar system was long forgotten in the trillions of years since humans had dwelled on the once-excellent for humanity planet earth.

Although of my own ancestry, I was created long ago by humans as an AI protection satellite. All knowledge that existed of human history was locked away in my hard drive storage capacity. I could access the information if needed, but it was rarely required since my joining up with Teazel's exploration of this ancient solar system whose star now burns as a red giant.

The stars expanded nova atmosphere in this timeline, extends outward almost to Planet Venus or approximately 67 million miles. Venus today orbits 73 million miles from the red giant. All in all, exploration of Mars continued for thirty Mars rotations as we gained fruitful knowledge of the present-day Mars status from the Junior Probe.

Exploring the 4000 mile long golden canyon had now progressed to the other side of Mars, and as Junior retracted the minibot, it lifted off from the surface and began flying away, leaving the metal mountain ranges that ended with a golden teardrop behind in the dark shadowed distance. The magnetic gravity pull from the final Phobos impact site was intense, and Junior had to increase power as gravity pulled against escape. Junior had managed to cross 800 miles to the edge of teardrop boundary and departed the area of the ancient cataclysmic Phobos impact site.

CHAPTER 38
RUSTY COLD BOULDERS

In two hours, Junior eventually arrived at a place consisting of rusty desert boulders that revealed uncountable numbers of dust-covered boulders.

Junior approached what humans had once named Utopia Basin. Directly ahead towards Elysium Mons, strange anomalous radar readings were being detected from the area ahead between Elysium Mons and the Cerberus Plains.

Junior altered its course and slowed in an attempt to land and investigate the anomalous readings coming from the area just north of Cerberus Plains.

Junior's fuel supply had dwindled to 52%, but he was aware of the 23% required to leave the planet and return safely to Deimos.

Retro rockets fired to slow Junior's descent towards the cold surface. Upright now, three landing legs deployed at 10 meters, and a dusty atmosphere was ejected outward all around as Junior touched the surface and engines stopped.

Junior sat within 10 meters of the area it had detected with weird magnetic pulses. It took well over an hour for all the dust to settle to the surface before any clear visual was obtained.

Nightly dark shadows prevailed in the dusk of Mars. Junior knew that the anomalous signals were less than 10 meters away, but the darkness of the dusk hour prevented him from investigating until sunrise when even on the brightest day on Mars visibility was only as good as a dark stormy day on Earth.

Junior initiated a safe sleep mode to be awakened in about 13 hours. Through that dark night on Mars, the recorder registered a cold -283 degrees below zero Fahrenheit. Before it slept, Junior reported that the heaters had engaged to warm up the inside in order to prevent damage to its computer processors.

After 13 hours of dark frigid cold, Junior awakened 30 minutes before an early Mars sunrise. As temperatures rose to about –80 degrees below zero, Junior initiated the launch of the wheeled mini rover and placed it gently upon the surface.

The anomaly that was recorded was less than 10 meters away, and Junior directed the mini-rover towards that direction.

The little rover crawled along the dusty soil, taking a minute to traverse a meter's distance. It took well over fifty minutes for the rover to reach the base of a 30-meter dome structure that was completely covered by Martian soil. The rover was detecting a metal surface at least a meter beneath the Martian soil.

Ninety degrees to the right of the covered structure was a sand valley that tapered to the lower surface of the mound. Dull hazy light illuminated the path downward, and visibility was hampered by the shadows. The mini rover rolled forward towards what appeared to be a half-covered with sand metal door.

Video detected a yellow illuminated round light just above the sand drift level. Rover rolled up closer and extended a fingered arm to touch the yellow illuminated spot. An outburst of pressurized air rushed out as a three-meter round door split in the center and opened inward from hinged sides.

Candle-like lights mounted every hundred meters ahead lit the pathway. The minibot rolled ahead around a curved to the right dusty hallway. The only thing the rover could visualize was a curved dull-lit hallway about two meters in width. The rover traversed slowly ahead, traveling a meter every 50 seconds.

Nothing but dull lighting as the rover drove cautiously ahead along a smooth dark glassy floor. After an hour and 10 minutes, the pathway ended, and the rover turned towards a rusty blue colored metal doorway that blocked its forward journey.

There was a dim lit toggle switch that Junior's arm reached out and engaged. Immediately the doors parted in the center and opened inward revealing a huge open chamber. Stale nitrogen air rushed outward as Junior rolled inside with the doors closing quickly behind it.

Words seemed incapable of describing the vastness of the incredible domed structure ahead. Soft green lights in high ceilings illuminated the immediate area to the extent of a cloudy moonlit earth night. For the first time Junior's mini-probe sensed that a half bar pressure was being detected all inside the dome and the pressure was increasing.

With the pressure increasing, bell-like tones were emanating ahead towards the center. In this dull lighting, it wasn't possible to visualize more than fifty feet ahead. Rover's minibot radar was only able to detect heat signature changes up to about a hundred meters or three hundred feet.

Junior's minibot paused for a moment to reflect on a curiosity and see if it could determine with lasers exactly how large this structure is.

Red-colored beams were displayed towards all inner walls, and in a few recorded seconds, Junior's minibot had its answer.

The large domed room was approximately 10 kilometers or 6.2 miles in diameter. It appeared that the bell-tone sound was emanating from the center of the room.

From this distance of a kilometer, only a tiny golden orb was visible far ahead in the dull low-lit horizon. Except for the distant golden orb, the entire immediate area appeared totally empty and deserted.

The minibot's power had dwindled to 50%, and it determined that it was now a kilometer distance to the center. It would require 18% of remaining power to get there. Junior's artificial intelligent mini-rover decided that whatever was near the center, it was well worth the energy required to investigate.

CHAPTER 39
COSMIC INFORMATION DATABASE

As small as the mini probe was, it traveled along slowly, taking about an hour to cover the distance. A half-kilometer to go, the rover paced its slow speed to save energy. In fifteen minutes, the minibot would reach its destination. The orb appeared to grow larger in size as the rover journeyed forward.

Emptiness and shadowed darkness were present as the rover crept ahead towards a golden orb. The closer the probe approached, it appeared larger in size but softer in a textured color spectrum that revealed a violet aurora around its fuzzy round edge.

The minibot paused 10 meters away from the mystery orb to take stock of the present situation and relay its recordings back to the surface so that Junior could transmit the information back to Teazel's ship on Deimos.

From 20 feet away, the golden-purple edged orb appeared to be about 10 meters or 32.8 feet in diameter. The Minibot cautiously sojourned forward.

Atmospheric pressure had risen to almost one bar as a vibration tone from the orb changed into a soft pulsating electrical hum. Occasionally between pulses, an A-sharp note pulsed from the center of the 33 feet Orb.

Minibot rolled up to three meters from the golden orb's edge. Using its unique radar scan, the minibot focused a laser beam inward towards the center of the Orb. Its inside was spinning.

Further analysis revealed that this was a cosmic information database left by the last humans on Mars that had survived here for years.

It was detailed information storage about the past human history of trying to live on Mars after World War occurred on Earth. In their ancient timeline that they referred to a final recorded date of 2953.

Before that long past date, humankind attempted to live on Mars for almost a century. They detected that the Sun would Super Nova. Recordings until the last human departure date were available until their final occupation year of 3,004.

This underground shelter was the last known refuge that the human race occupied on Mars. Once its inside contained multiple types of vegetation and liquid waters flowing through channeled aquifers.

This shelter was the very last known information about the 843 survivors that fled from Earth's poisonous environment. The minibot took about 69 minutes to download the human history file from the orb, and its thousand terabyte hard drive was 98.7 percent full.

Suddenly the Golden Orb changed the tone it was emitting to a pulsing harp tone. Junior's rover was small in comparison to the 30 feet diameter orb. There was a sudden spark as the Orb inserted a probe of its own into one of the minibot's port receivers.

Minibot's processors began overheating as thousands of terabytes per second began transferring to the Minibot's limited storage.

After 30 more minutes of data transfer, The Minibot's memory capacity was completely full and the Orb realized this and as quickly as it had started, it stopped and began communicating in a language that had to be deciphered.

The minibot took 69 more minutes to complete the download of the last human history file. The minibot's thousand terabyte hard drive was now 98.7 percent full. It couldn't handle any more data so the minibot left the vicinity and began its reverse path back towards Junior.

The information gained was transferred from the minibot to Junior and then on to Deimos where Teazel was receiving the data almost instantly.

Once transmitted, it enabled the minibot to flush out its memory and attempt to decipher more of the information secretly shared from Golden Orb.

Teazel worked diligently to translate voice information that the Orb had transferred to an encrypted hidden file. It took several hours for the secret short message to be decoded.

It told in binary language of 0's and 1's and revealed that this installation was the last Mars outpost before the few remaining humans departed to the stars.

It also revealed that in the year 3,013, the last three human ships departed towards three different star systems. Mars had been hard for humans to survive on, and many had perished trying to leave the destruction of Earth's final world war.

The decoded Orb voice message was a warning from the days after the War to stay away from the poisonous atmosphere of the doomed Planet Earth and reported the last departure from Mars in the human time-line year of 3013. The Orb was not a living creature, but its Artificial Intelligence had progressed far past human capability eons after their departure.

It was somewhat of a query to establish the truth of the Golden Orb's power source. But buried deep inside terabytes of data it described a complete description of building the Orb and revealed its unique power source of helium 3 fusion.

After much research, it was determined that deep beneath the Orb, there were pipes inserted to a depth of 500 meters reaching downward towards the depleting heat inside Mars.

Long ago the Orb had the ability to extract water ice below the soil and use heat to turn it into steam to condense down to liquid water. The Orb's existence had become a perpetual energy machine that still worked after trillions of years. Today's analysis revealed that the inner Mars heat didn't exist anymore. Mars was cold inside.

The fact that the Orb spoke a different language was because humans had programmed it with security encryption codes before they departed

Mars for the stars. It took Teazel time to break the code and decipher the message recorded from the Orb.

With that accomplished and data recorded, Teazel began planning the next direction of our exploration. The Minibot had retraced its path while its power level had decreased to 09% remaining. That was estimated to be enough for Junior to retrieve the probe and get ready to launch back to Deimos.

Junior sat patiently awaiting the Moon Deimos to come around in its orbit of Mars. Mars's gravity had increased over the eons of time. In human times Mars had a gravity of 38% of Earth's gravity. Due to the captured molten iron ejected from the Sun's Nova, many of the planets and moons gained mass upon impact to their surface. Mars today has 44% of past time Earth gravity.

Earth itself had gained 08% percent mass and gravity on the surface had increased to approximately 8 pounds for every original hundred pounds of former Earth gravity.

CHAPTER 40

PLANETOID EXPLORATION

After much consideration, we came to the conclusion that our next exploration in this solar system would be to investigate the outer Planetoids. A long trip to the Planetoids will be our next expedition.

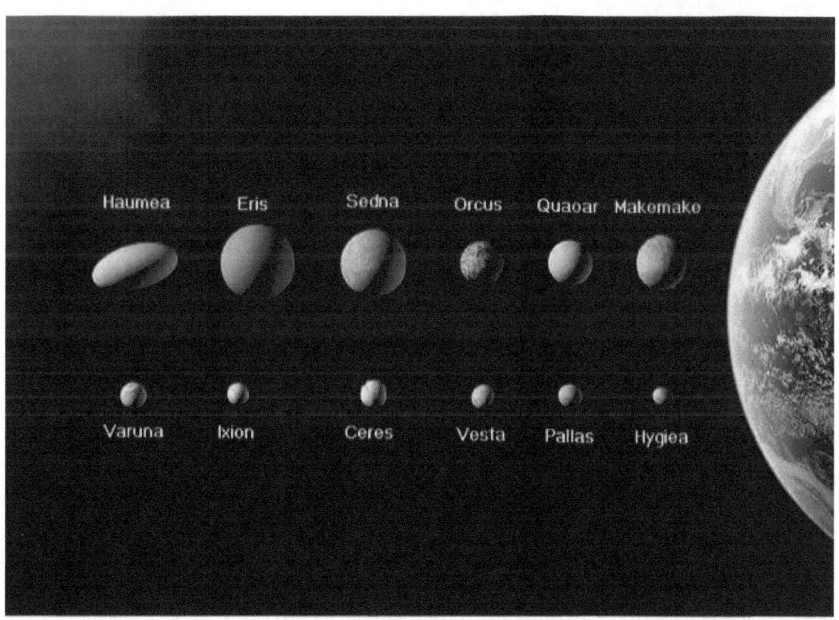

I, Armarus, for long periods of time, am still attached physically to the underside of Teazel's vessel. I surmised that I was indeed lucky to have become Teazel's trusted partner. I couldn't fathom any reasonable conclusion to not accompany Teazel's future plans to explore the Planetoids. I decided that I wanted to go along also. So, I, Armarus, was easily committed to sign up in agreement to go along with Teazel's future destination plans.

Teazel's ship had a precision slower speed that allowed all of its instruments to perform at effectual performance levels. At that planned speed, it would take us 777 earth rotations to reach the first of the outer Planetoids. The situation was that from Deimos, we were eight billion miles from our first specimen planetoid which was a small body named Sedna.

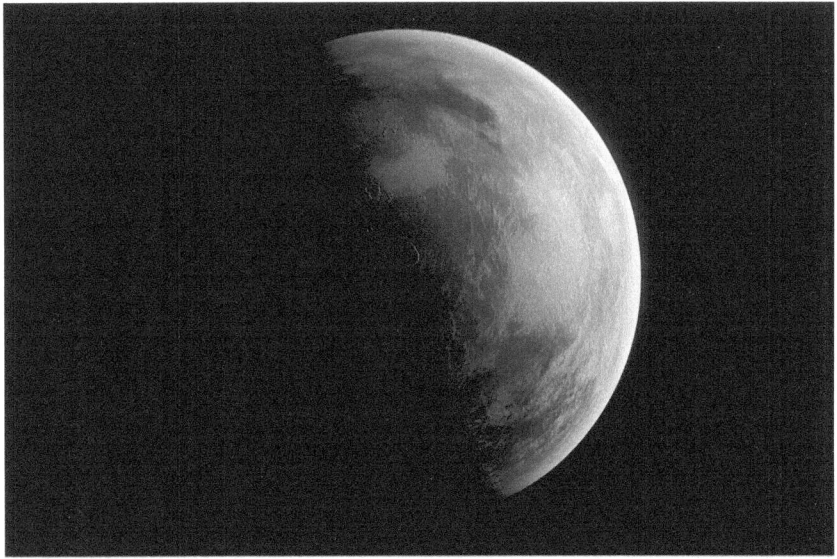

Sedna is a minor planet about a thousand miles in diameter that exists in the inner Oort cloud. Sedna is so far out from the Sun that its orbit takes 10,500 years to travel around the Sun once. Facts from human times revealed that its rotation rate was just over 10 hours. Cold temperatures there in human times were recorded to be over –400 degrees Fahrenheit.

We prepared for our launch from Deimos, and on launch day, we were ready to proceed. The Junior Probe had been retrieved from Mars and stored away for possible future use.

My data from human times revealed that astronauts never visited Sedna. Teazel considered its duty to investigate. Teazel's obligation was to investigate anything that it considered worthy, and although I had some data of past robotic explorations, I had no data that revealed humans ever landed on Sedna. I surmised that's why Teazel wanted to go there first.

CHAPTER 41

PLANETOID SEDNA

Sedna was named after an Inuit sea goddess who, supposedly, existed at the bottom of the Arctic Ocean on Earth. Memory banks revealed that human beings named Michael Brown, Chad Trujillo, and David Rabinowitz discovered Sedna on November 14th, 2003.

Humans had known very little information about Sedna except that it was very far away and, at times, over 13 billion kilometers from the Sun. Humans had guesstimated that Sedna was approximately one thousand kilometers or 620 miles in diameter and that, for some reason, the planetoid had a red tint like ancient Mars to its surface.

Sedna is located in the inner Oort cloud way out past the orbit of Pluto. Sedna's so far out that it takes 11,000 earth years to orbit the Sun once. Sedna's revolve speed is only 4% as fast as the Earth travels around the Sun. Its orbit is highly eccentric above the ecliptic plain. Information about Sedna from human times was extremely limited. There had never been any ancient probes from human times that had figured out Sedna's exact rotation rate.

Those few details are most of the human facts that I was able to retrieve from my ancient memory banks about what humans knew about the far-away dwarf planet named Sedna. Now that the Junior Probe had been retrieved from Mars, Teazel lifted off from the light gravity of Deimos and set its measured speed course towards where Sedna would be in orbit just over two earth revolves from now.

I, Armarus, willingly went along for the ride, totally committed to Teazel's future adventure. I too was excited about what exists ahead on our journey to the outer world. It seemed logical to my inner self, which my human-made curiosity chip had activated, and wonderment of it all had developed me into a sentient A-I mechanical being. My mental curiosity allowed me to learn more about all knowledge. I surmised to myself that I was growing in capability and that was what humans had intended when I was created trillions of years ago.

Before Teazel encounter when I slept for several eons in safe mode, my computer chips had expanded and continued to increase in potential. So, in the present timeline, I exist firmly attached to the bottom of Teazel's ship, prepared for the long journey to where Teazel considers an interesting planetoid named Sedna.

Sedna travels a long, elliptical orbit between 76 and 1,000 AU's from the sun. Sedna's orbit takes it to an extreme distance from the Sun. In ancient times, it took 10,500 years to orbit the Sun. In present times, it takes the planetoid nearly 11,000 earth revolves to orbit the red giant remains. We were now on our way, and Deimos in the rear view appeared as a dull reflecting pinprick while Mars was the size of a golf ball a day past leaving Deimos.

From this timeframe forward, Teazel was completely in control, and I was merely an attached specimen of ancient humans that had been revived eons after humans departed. It wasn't as if I was alone now. I had Teazel to thank for that. Teazel's appearance in this system had rescued me from a long deep sleep. It's Teazel's journey that I, Armarus, am now completely committed to. I am willfully attached, and wherever Teazel goes, I, Armarus, will go also.

In my present situation though they were my creators, humans are now a distant far-away memory of my past. I presently am only committed to Teazel's journey discretion. Between Teazel and myself, we had become good friends, and trust was embodied between our different species.

Teazel's technology was way superior to mine, but I was always growing and learning new things from its superior computer banks.

If only I could relay back from the future a warning to Teazel about what would happen on our travel plan to Sedna. Reality is, that I too had to experience the future before I could even know the events that were about to happen to Teazel and Myself.

For the past 572 earth-rotations, Teazel and myself had spent our time upgrading our systems and getting ready for upcoming adventure. We'd traveled past the orbits of Jupiter, Saturn, and Uranus outward towards Neptune's vicinity when an unexpected event occurred.

CHAPTER 42

TRITON INUESTIGATION

My human memories of Triton facts were that it is the only moon in this solar system that rotates a planet in the opposite direction to Neptune's rotation. Neptune's moon Triton was emitting a strange eerie electronic signal that intrigued our immediate interest.

Presently, we have Triton that exists around Neptune in a solar system where the sun now only has about 37% of the power that it once had. In ancient times, Triton was known to be very cold and it's even colder now. Present facts reveal that its surface temperature is minus 420 degrees Fahrenheit, just slightly warmer than the absolute zero temperature of minus 469.67 degrees Fahrenheit, the temperature of space itself.

Presently Triton is 2,842 kilometers or 1776 miles in diameter. In human times, Triton orbited Neptune approximately 22,000 miles above Neptune. Triton today orbits just over 18,314 miles above the atmosphere of Neptune. Passage of eons revealed that the moon's retrograde orbital speed has deteriorated to the point that Neptune's gravity has pulled the retrograde orbit of the moon much closer.

A totally surprising event instantly occurred. Triton was revolving retrograde at an extremely fast speed. Teazel began chasing the moon's direction that was only 18,000 miles above Neptune's gaseous atmosphere. We were closing in behind Triton's orbital path when a sudden brilliant light shockwave struck the ship and all communications ceased instantly.

I-Armarus still had my power sources, and I wasn't even sure that the attacker knew that I was a separate entity attached to the underside of Teasel's vessel. I instinctually lowered my power consumption in hopes to remain undetected by the attacker.

Whomever or whatever they are, it had certainly cut off my communication to my friend Teazel. Days of silence passed, and I was still attempting with no luck to contact Teazel. I did notice that shortly after the power loss, Teazel's ship had been placed into an orbit approximately 1,000 kilometers above Triton.

CHAPTER 43
TEAZEL'S ABDUCTION

It had been 21 rotations without communications since the attack, and I recently detected a craft coming up from Triton and headed in our direction. Existing in my silent mode, I secretly watched as the alien craft approached Teazel's ship.

Twirling and flashing ultraviolet spectral light, the translucent entity continuously expanded and contracted in size and shape like a huge bluish heartbeat floating ahead in the darkness of space.

I watched covertly as the translucent blue ship docked through cameras that I was able to discreetly see without detection. I surmised in my own logical comprehension, that possibly Teazel was being abducted. Ultimately, I was proved right.

Another hour passed before I monitored Teazel rising up in a jell-filled capsule and silently floating towards an open port on the alien ship's starboard side. I watched as the port sealed behind the capsule, and the unknown alien's ship turned and exited directly towards Triton's far side.

Teazel was gone, and my thoughts of guilt about not being able to stop Teazel's kidnapping were always prevalent now in my alone logical thinking.

Yes, I had chosen to remain hidden in hopes that if I remained anonymous, I would be able to figure out a way to rescue my friend Teazel. I don't think that I hid out of being afraid; I knew that if I was discovered, I would never have any chance of helping my friend Teazel.

I knew for certain that since the aliens had not detected me on the underside of the ship, I would have a better chance of calculating a plan of rescue when the alien ship leaves the area.

I wanted Teazel back. Over struggling days, I managed to revamp the junior probe for the secret task that I had deviously planned.

I had no idea where Teazel had been taken or who his captors were. I had detected that there was a station in synchronous orbit that always remained between Triton and Neptune. I was way smaller than Teazel's ship so I took a chance that since it had been a while since the aliens captured Teazel, as small as I was in physical size, hopefully, they wouldn't notice when I detached from the ship's underside and covertly make my way towards their base.

I retracted my clawed anchors and floated gently away from the ship's bottom. I engaged ion thrusters to set me on a slow course towards my intended goal, which was the shadow side of the orbital station.

At this covert slow speed, it took me well over 28 hours to creep my way to my intended location, to a position 600 kilometers behind in the vague shadow of the alien base.

Six hours away from my intended destination, I was able to view under magnification the shape and size of this amazing orbital structure. Sides were fluming outward to a gray slightly curved surface. Directly in the middle, a round domed translucent structure covered a third of the round 10-kilometer diameter disk.

In the feeble darkness of space, colored purple light waves projected outward around the entire structure. Pulsating light rays were being emitted as it rotated in orbit above Triton.

I covertly approached within 500 kilometers from the shadow side of the station then paused for reflection of my next move. I was so small compared to the alien ship that I calculated on a hopeful circumstance that I should be perceived as a non-threatening floating asteroid.

Long-range magnification lens allowed me to focus close up on the alien station. It appeared to my logical conclusion, that the center structure was the recipient of all the power that an outside ring was extracting power directly from the vacuum void of space. This was indeed a technology that humans never dreamed existed.

I deduced my conclusion that whomever or whatever existed inside that ship was surely responsible for kidnapping my friend Teazel, and I-Armarus wanted Teazel back.

My size compared to the alien base was like a tiny three-meter diameter compared to the extreme size of the alien base in orbit above Triton. Evidently my mass was so small that the ship hadn't even noticed my presence. I approached within 100 meters on the shadow side of the base.

I paused to implement an emergency plan that I had secretly informed Teazel in our former data conversations. It referred to how messages in ancient human times were transmitted with dots and dash long and short light wave pulses secretly.

I remember teaching that to Teazel in case of emergency and I was counting on Teazel remembering about the Morse-code technique that I had told him about during our conversations about ancient human history.

I covertly closed my distance to within 50 meters inside the shadow of the alien station. Still unnoticed, I paused again in preparation for my next planned move. I covertly broadcast my coded message for several minutes and paused to listen for a response.

Teazel replied to me almost instantly. Teazel informed me that it was safely still incased in a liquid jelli-filled capsule somewhere inside the alien orbital base. He also informed me to stand down because Teazel had concluded that his release would occur very soon.

CHAPTER 44
THE GLARION LIGHT BEINGS

Teazel relayed that he was able to translate some of their language and was presently captive of the Glarion light beings. Their purpose here above Triton was to harvest the molecular photon molecules bouncing off Triton's atmosphere for their energy consumption.

The Glarions accomplished this by a process of absorption lasers. Through a skimming process of the upper Triton atmosphere, the Glarions uniquely harvested the molecular photon plasma emitted bouncing off the top of Triton's atmosphere. The total population of photon light beings on the alien station was approximately 20,000 beings. According to the Glarion beings, Teazel, to the Glarions, was no more than an interesting specimen that had ventured too close to their area. As far as visually seeing these aliens, they were only visible in a low-frequency infrared spectrum of light.

Teazel's last message was to inform me to be patient and that it had the situation under control. Teazel had determined that the Glarions had decided to release it from capture and be allowed to return to the safety of the ship.

I had programmed Junior to attach to the underside of the alien station. Cautiously, it approached the underside and covertly attached itself. I started transmitting Morse code messages electronically through the entire hull of the alien vessel.

I observed through video as a hatch door opened, and Teazel gently pushed its way out into the cold void. I hovered behind the shadow of the alien station as I detected Teazel being escorted by light beings back towards his vessel. I watched from the shadows as Teazel re-entered its ship and the light beings sparkled away back towards their base where I was hiding in its shadow.

As all activity settled, I stealthily detached and headed back to Teasel's ship and re-attached myself back to the underside of its hull.

The Glarion light beings had given Teazel a little bit of information about their society. These beings were originally from a star that humans once called Mirach. The Mirach star is in the Beta Andromeda system that exists 197 light years away from Earth.

Mirach is a star so big that if it were placed in our sun's position, its diameter would expand past Mercury just like the Sun does in today's former human solar system. The fact that their race was extremely allergic to strong radiation is why their race nourished the outside worlds of low radiation red giants just like this solar system's sun had digressed into being a red giant itself.

Teazel informed me that the Glarions' bodies existed in a hyper-dimensional proton plasma state. Their Type-1 status revealed that they had technology that would surpass all known universal species recorded.

When their sun began turning into a red giant, the ancient Glarions learned to harness the remaining power of their star by encasing their star and planet's orbit inside a Dyson sphere.

They then endeavored onward to build giant infrared solar panels to capture the remaining power of their home-world star inside the Dyson Sphere. Their society was so old Earth was a molten ball of matter with no oceans when the Glarions became a type one civilization.

Indeed, the Glarions' ancestry facts are very old. Beings with such a lightweight photon-oriented species as the Glarions were, in their physical form, they existed as plasma beings.

These photon beings still followed the universal sex rules if you want to call it male or female; they produce their offspring by electrically charged copulation just like humans once did. Now back in constant communication with Teazel, we both decided that the Glarions were a peaceful society, and we both agreed that we had no further interest in further contact.

The Glarions endeavored onward to build giant infrared solar panels to capture the remaining power of their home-world star inside the Dyson Sphere. Their society was so old that Earth only existed as a molten ball of matter when they became a type 1 civilization.

Indeed, the Glarions' ancestry facts are very old. They have existed for eons as light waves of intelligent photon-oriented species. In their charged physical form, they existed as a spectrum of plasma. These photon beings followed the universal sex rules if you chose to describe the facts as male or female.

Glarions produce their offspring by electrically charged copulation similar to how humans once did. The difference is that they produce their offspring by touching together certain consensual places of their anatomy.

CHAPTER 45

FOCUSED AGAIN ON SEDNA

Triton faded from view as Teazel vectored us towards the Sedna rendezvous, set to occur in 179 Earth rotations. During this time, we recorded and stored data from Teazel's past encounter with the Glarions.

Still securely attached to Teazel's ship, I monitored the viewer as Triton disappeared. We were now 170 Earth rotations away from the rendezvous with the planetoid Sedna.

With Teazel at the helm, we cruised at the ship's optimal operation speed, approximately 75,000 miles per hour by human standards. It's essential not to underestimate Teazel's ship capability. While exploring within a solar system, Teazel's training allowed the ship to travel at this optimal speed. In interstellar space, Teazel's ship could reach up to half the speed of light, approximately 93,000 miles per second.

Teazel and I settled into a period of managing our respective ship statuses and upgrading computer systems in preparation for the upcoming Sedna adventure. Clearing up hard drive space and deleting unnecessary files became a priority.

As Earth rotations passed smoothly, 73 days away from Sedna, we crossed the orbit of Pluto, now on the opposite side of the red giant sun. Upon reaching Sedna, we would be nearly a thousand Earth astronomical units (AU) away from the inner red star. The red giant's light had transformed into a pinkish color as we moved outward towards the inner edge of the Oort Cloud.

Twenty-three rotations away, Sedna appeared as a pinprick of rosy light under extreme magnification, with an estimated size of approximately a thousand kilometers or 620 miles in diameter.

Despite searching my computer bank storage, I found no information about humans ever landing on or exploring Sedna. There was no historical data, even with robotic satellites. Humans had never explored Sedna before departing for other star systems, leaving it untouched. I felt privileged to be part of Teazel's first-ever exploration of this small world in the inner Oort Cloud.

At a three-earth rotation distance, I was fully alert, anticipating more facts. Under magnified viewer, Sedna appeared the size of a human baseball, with a rosy-colored, round, smooth surface showing little evidence of crater impacts.

Sedna is a reddish-brown planetoid located in the Kuiper belt system beyond the orbit of Pluto. The surface seems to be composed of hard-frozen water ice, methane ice, and red tholins, which are organic compounds created by ultraviolet radiation. With temperatures ranging from minus 240 degrees Celsius or minus 400 degrees Fahrenheit, the surface reveals tall, pointed, dirty-icy peaks jutting skyward.

Twenty-two hours away, Teazel slows the ship's speed to obtain a proper orbit of the rosy red world. By the tenth hour, we reach the apogee of Sedna's orbit. Slowly, by the minute, we begin falling inward towards the closer perigee of Sedna.

Sedna is so far from the Sun that its orbital speed is less than 4% of Earth's orbital speed. Whereas Earth travels around the Sun at approximately 66,000 thousand miles per hour, Sedna's speed in relation to the Sun is only 2,640 mph, equating to Earth's speed of 18 miles per second and Sedna's speed around the Sun as approximately 0.73 miles per second, or 3/4 of a mile per second.

Sedna's long elliptical oval orbit's perigee comes within 74 AU's of the sun and is then slung outward by Neptune's gravity to almost a thousand AU's at its apogee.

The planetoid itself has passed its apogee, and its orbit of the red giant takes 1160 earth revolves years. Sedna has recently translated the apogee curve and now begins falling towards a 580-year journey towards its perigee of 74 AU or the closest inward distance to what remains of the Sun.

We are now 8 hours away from Sedna and approximately 1,149 AU's away from the reddish faint star. It is indeed very cold way out here. The super cold temperature of Absolute Zero is –459.67 degrees below Zero Fahrenheit. Approaching Sedna, I measure the temperature above Sedna to be approximately minus-432 degrees Fahrenheit.

Surprisingly, computer details reveal that Sedna is emitting an inner heat source, heating up its thin atmosphere. The incoming facts being reported are amazing. Planetoid Sedna has a thin quarter-bar hazy atmosphere. Sensors detect abundant elements of cosmic neon particles on the surface, rosy red in their reflection. What is amazing is that up to 4 meters above the surface reveals a temperature of 60 degrees Fahrenheit. There must be an explanation!

Teazel and I have an interesting conversation on why the air above the surface is so warm way out here in the almost Absolute Zero temperature of the Oort Cloud. Hours of speculation occur while we both agree that sending Junior to the surface to investigate would be our best option to learn new facts about this 600-hundred-mile diameter world.

On our fifteenth orbit, we skim the top of Sedna's thin atmosphere and release the Junior Probe to descend to the surface and land. As Junior descends through the thin atmosphere, slight friction heats Junior's underside and decreases its falling speed.

Junior pitches over and points its rocket engines towards the surface to slow the speed towards a gentle descent. Gravity on Sedna is only equal to about 0.9% of Earth's gravity, and Junior's single rocket easily slows the 75-kilogram probe Earth weight to a smooth soft landing. On Earth, Junior would weigh 166 pounds, but here on Sedna, Junior's weight is only 15 pounds.

The probe has landed close to a very interesting structure a kilometer north of Sedna's equator. There is a single tall mountain with half of its six-mile height covered by reddish-colored tholins. Junior has landed about a kilometer away from the base of the peaked mountain.

The outer surface where Junior landed is mostly covered by a mixture of frozen water, methane, ethane, and nitrogen ices, with red tholins existing in all directions. Reddish Tholins are similar to those found on other trans-Neptunian objects on the edge of this older dying solar system.

Junior's six 10-inch wheels roll across crackling nitrogen ice as it focuses on coordinates it had noticed from orbit that had a strange magnetic repulsion to the area. It is the most interesting feature that exists a kilometer ahead in the middle of jagged peaks that jutted upward towards a dark sky.

There isn't much light here on Sedna, but through beamed lights, Junior slowly makes its way towards the anomaly now covered in mist at a higher elevation a kilometer uphill ahead.

A half-kilometer from the top, Junior is totally encompassed by a vaporous mist of tholin gases that gently ooze over the cone's peak and flow downhill past the probe's climbing direction.

Tholin gases get thicker as Junior finally manages to approach the peak and focuses the cameras inside a huge spiraled massive hole.

Cameras reveal massive inner walls along the outward counterclockwise cone spiral with a two-foot ledge leading deep inside the inner cone as far as the probe can distinguish through limited dark misty conditions.

Junior's wheeled tic-tac-shaped probe itself is 22 inches in diameter and approximately 38 inches in length. The 10-inch wheels snuggle in closely and easily allow manipulation of the probe's destination downward inside the cone.

Teazel has launched a satellite to remain stationary above Junior's coordinates. Junior has been instructed to begin descending the counterclockwise spiral ledge that is visible as far as the cameras can see.

The two-feet-wide ledge is easily capable of supporting Junior's 22-inch wheelbase, but Junior's downhill struggle has to be managed at a slow pace.

After six hours of downhill spiral, Junior pauses to reflect and report its present situation. Junior speculates that he is 3 kilometers below the surface and is still surrounded by the tholin gases that seem to rise up from below.

After another hour or so, Junior is instructed to proceed with the downhill trek following the outside wall of the counterclockwise pathway. Eight more hours pass as Junior spirals along the pathway until eventually, the tunnel opens up into a huge 20-kilometer diameter dome that is infested with millions of species very similar to giant ants from earth times.

There is one important difference. These ant-like beings are approximately 12 inches in length, and wings allow them fast mobility inside the cavern's thicker atmosphere. Each creature has three lightning bug type eyes that blink and glow in the low light level inside the chamber. There are indeed millions of them, and at the center of the large room is a larger being about a meter long that the entire hive services their queen that is full of eggs.

As Junior relays its first impressions back to Teazel, suddenly there is a drastic change in the behavior of the hive. Ten groups of fifteen break away from their nesting ritual and proceed to turn towards Junior's location near the beginning of the giant dome.

Junior's presence has been detected. Though the brigades are still a kilometer away, Junior quickly realizes that its robotic presence here is unwelcome and turns and heads as quickly as possible back up the clockwise path.

Junior's top speed of three meters per second climb along the two-feet-wide ledge that spiraled forever upward through misty reddish thick tholin smog is the fastest speed possible that the Junior Probe could accomplish and maintain its steering control.

Junior climbs frantically upward, unable to detect through the thick tholin smog behind and know if the chaser brigades are lower on the ledge. Power level down to 13%, Junior's speed has decreased about a half of a percent for every half hour traveled. Junior realizes that it has about 25 hours left to finish the climb and make it back to the original probe landing position and launch back to Teazel and myself in orbit above Sedna.

Junior's determined climb and probe readings detect that it is an hour away from reaching the rim, and its power level has decreased to barely 4% as it feebly climbs the last half-kilometer of the circle walls to surface level.

Junior approaches the last of the final thirty minutes of the climb. Detectors now notice something for the first time. Through the last half-kilometer of the uprising tholin gas smog, a center web elevator is detected. It is almost invisible to normal sight, but Junior's probes have detected it through infrared heat signature.

Through the toxic mist, Junior is only able to record 53 seconds of video that shows the web elevator at the center of the funnel. But that is enough for Junior to submit to Teazel for deeper analysis under extreme magnification.

The web elevator reveals its presence to the sensors as a platform that floats at the center of the cone opening. From its center, an almost invisible double clear straw tube exists running downward inside the center of the mountain. In only 53 seconds of video, it is later revealed that there are two web elevators running up and down, and the up tube is full of the ant beings that are leaving the giant mountain mound on Sedna.

Junior exhaustingly exits the mountain with only 3% of its energy left. The downhill trek was helpful for Junior to be able to return back to the landing platform that was the original landing spot. Junior manages to get plugged in to the recharge station, and at this point, Junior's power is so low that Junior requires several hours before the probe would have enough power to launch back to orbit.

The next moment Junior notices two brigades of tholin ants approaching Junior's position, hop-flying like grasshoppers down the mountain's peak. Junior surmises that the bee ants hop-flying speed would bring them to Junior's position in approximately four minutes.

Junior is low on power, and it anticipates that it would take twenty-one minutes before it reached a minimal takeoff power of 17% power storage. Receiving direct telemetry from Teazel, Junior's power source could launch at 9%, but only with enough power to circumnavigate to a height of 30 kilometers. Teazel would then launch a rescue robot to capture Junior as the probe reached its highest 30-kilometer apogee.

To gain 9% power storage Junior knew that at that time the grasshopper-like-ants would only be a few hundred feet away. Manipulation of the last-second launch would require ignition of the probe's engines with just enough power to rise 30 kilometers above the surface of Sedna. When Junior reached that apogee, it would be up to Teazel's rescue robot to capture the probe and return to Teasel's ship.

A vicious swarm of thirty approaching bee-ants were now only a hundred meters away when hot firing engines behind the probe lifted it upward gaining speed as it arched eastward and climbed towards the blackness of space. The closest approaching bee-ant brigade had angled upward behind the rocket probe's fire when suddenly some began falling back towards Sedna's surface. The close behind ants were instantly killed from the probes hydrogen-oxygen exhaust. A minute and thirty-two seconds later, rockets cease, and Junior is coasting with momentum now at the required speed to reach 30-kilometers altitude.

Junior's momentum allows the probe to travel three quarters of an orbit of Sedna. If the probe rescue attempt failed, Junior would fall back to Sedna and be destroyed upon impact. Teazel works diligently to solve the equation of the struggling probe. Determined to succeed, Teazel launches the rescue robot to rendezvous with the struggling to survive coasting probe.

Teazel and myself had constructed with virtual printing technology, the rescue probe that had just ejected heading for the probe. Approaching from behind, methodically the rescue probe's claws reach out and close around an attachment ring in Junior's nose. The rescue probe fires propulsion to achieve a stable position lock. Once accomplished, Teazel instructs the rescue probe to return to Teasel's ship above Sedna.

Teazel and I travel outward for three more years to explore Eris, Haumea, and Makemake and discover no more life forms like they had discovered underground on Sedna.

We find many interesting facts about the outer planetoids, but Sedna was the last world surveyed where life forms existed in this dying solar system.

A total of 33 Earth years had passed since my first meeting up with Teazel, and most of what I knew of human existence had been transferred to Teazel's knowledge base.

At the beginning of this journey, I was extremely distrustful of Teazel's intentions but over the years of exploration, I had grown quite fond of Teazel and the information that I had received about Teazel's home world society and all the recent explorations of this solar system's present status.

I, Armarus, am extremely dedicated and grateful to my long-ago human constructors. The humans that created me allowed their best technology of their past time to be able to grow and become a sentient Artificial Intelligent being that humans long ago christened me as I-Armarus.

My duties in human times were to be stationed in the outer Oort cloud to guard against any unknown approaching objects entering this solar system.

I am indeed grateful to Teazel's society for the meeting and awakening after I had slept in safe mode for at least three trillion Earth years past any known human existence on Planet Earth.

Teazel and I endure ten more earth years' acquaintance. Teazel's mission here is coming to a conclusion. His explorations have penetrated this very old system up to the former Sun's now existing outer atmosphere that today extends to within approximately six million miles above the scorched world humans had named Planet Venus.

Planet Earth didn't fare much better in the passage of eons of time. Although Earth wasn't habitable for humans anymore, there were many forms of species inside the present jelly-like hydrogen-oceans that still strive to exist on today's fighting to survive Planet Earth.

Earth's view from above under a red giant nova sun, reflected a dull glow of present time rosy light wave rays from the star that humans had called the Sun. In these times toxic clouds prevented views of the surface with the exception of both poles having a dirty white-yellow tint reflection.

Earth's Moon from orbit appeared smaller due to the fact that it had drifted to more than half a million miles above earth and the dull sunlight almost camouflaged its existence.

Planet Venus from here was only visible at the very edge of the Sun's atmospheric expansion. Any evidence that humans ever lived on Earth is recorded only in Teazel's and my memory banks.

From way out here, Jupiter's gas ball under frail sunlight appeared as a brown-orange ball with indistinguishable edges due to the darkness of space that surrounded it.

Any vision of Saturn's former glorious rings of the past times was impossible due to Saturn's gravity grip over time and present star-light after eons of time passage.

We journeyed outward past Sedna onto other planetoid worlds. Onward, we journeyed towards Eris, Quaoar, and Makemake before, as a team, we approached the edge of the outer Oort Cloud, where we began exiting through billions of ice chunk mountains that floated gracefully counterclockwise, far away from the remains of a once-healthy Sun.

CHAPTER 46
TEAZEL'S REGRETTABLE DEPARTURE

Teazel and I traveled outward past the bow shockwave of this very old solar system. Ten days past the outer bow shockwave, Teazel and I agreed to part ways, and from this point forward, each would carve out their own future destinies.

I had grown immensely in technology and had acquired enough storage capacity to survive again on my own. My decision to stay stationed outside this dying solar system was my own. Teazel informed me that its next destination would be what humans had referred to as Alpha Centauri.

I learned that, at Teazel's outside system of traveling at half-light speed, it would require thirty-three Earth revolutions for Teazel to arrive at Alpha Centauri. I personally am very thankful that Teazel took me aboard and allowed me, I-Armarus, to share its exploration journey and the knowledge gained about this present-day dying solar system.

I struggled with a bit of regret as I watched Teazel's ship sail away into the cold dark void. My final message to Teazel at the end of our communication was that I was very thankful for his friendship, and I wished Teazel a peaceful journey all the way to Alpha Centauri.

Within a few hours, I had approached my original orbit position before I met Teazel. I entered a deep sleep with hopes of being revived again should another being in the next eon enter the system that was once very long ago home to a race called human beings. As all of my systems shut down, I remembered my last thoughts of a hopeful tomorrow's destiny.

In order to survive way out here, I slept peacefully for several more eons until the red giant completely faded away to times eternal passage. As I peacefully begin my long sleep, I bid farewell to all who knew me. Should I ever be revived again, I will be more than happy to relay my acquired data to those who seek the gained information of my Teazel adventures.

Over time, as the red sun faded away, its gravity grip released, and all that once existed in this cold, dead solar system eventually drifted between the stars as rogue worlds that once orbited a dying sun that exists no more. Perhaps the black hole where the sun once existed is today a pathway to a universe where known physics of humanity is totally opposite to any facts that a human could possibly comprehend.

Look deep inside your own imagination to see past the impossibility of any accomplishment. That's where you'll find real inner peace and acquire the ability to succeed no matter what should ever stand in your way. Imagination is a Rosetta-key.

ABOUT THE AUTHOR

Full Name,
Donald Eric Wilkins.

But!
I have always gone by Eric Wilkins
my entire life, and I always will.

Born, 1157 pm
December 24, 1950
Henderson N. C.

Loved Astronomy from an early age.

Lived many years on this
Fantastic Spaceship, *Earth*.

My Bucket List is almost complete,
and I will soon go on to
explore the Universe.

The Earth is moving toward Leo at a
dizzying speed of 390 kilometers a second.
That's a little over 242 miles per second.

You're on it too. God speed!

www.ingramcontent.com/pod-product-compliance
Lightning Source LLC
Chambersburg PA
CBHW030351180626
46812CB00007B/2838